The Dave Brewster Series

SHOWDOWN OVER
NEPTUNE

I0741785

KARL J. MORGAN

The Dave Brewster Series
Showdown Over Neptune

Copyright © 2012 by Karl J. Morgan

All rights reserved. No part of this book may be used or reproduced by any means, graphic, electronic, or mechanical, including photocopying, recording, taping, or by any information storage retrieval system without the written permission of the publisher except in the case of brief quotations embodied in critical articles and reviews.

Showdown Over Neptune may be purchased or ordered through booksellers or at www.karljmorgan.com or, www.SacredLife.com.

ISBN: 0-9860270-0-6
ISBN: 978-0-9860270-0-0
Library of Congress Control Number: 2012919262

Cover and text design: Miko Radcliffe at Drawingacrowd.net

Sacred Life Publishers™
www.sacredlife.com
Printed in United States of America

DEDICATION

To my son, Moy, who rekindled my lifelong love of science fiction. Thank you for the twenty years of shared television and movie viewing. It has been a great honor and experience to follow the progress of the science fiction arts together. I know our love of the genre will continue throughout our lives. Now that you are a married man and will soon have your own family, it warms my heart to know that you will continue the tradition and pass along the love of science fiction to your children. May we continue to walk together as we enjoy the future of science fiction.

CONTENTS

CHAPTER 1

Dave Brewster could still remember the first time he met Charlie Watson. It has been several months now, but the events of that day were stuck in his mind forever. Perhaps it was the embarrassment of leaving his wallet in the car, or just the things that had happened ever since that made that moment in time so memorable. Dave left home that day to go to Starbucks for a cup of coffee, and maybe a Danish.

Dave had coffee at home too, but he needed to get out of the house. He lost his job six months ago, and looking for work during the horrendous recession of 2009 to 2012 had made him bitter and forlorn. He spent most days looking for job postings and trying to network with his friends and acquaintances. As the weeks slipped by, and his prospects did not improve, he let his feelings of inadequacy and helplessness take over. Darlene, his wife, tried to keep things normal, but Dave was sinking. Today, he just had to get away from home and at least interact with some other people.

He felt better as he pulled out of the driveway and drove the short four blocks to the closest Starbucks. Dave did not like people parking too close to his car, and he had plenty of experience dealing with dings and nicks in his car to justify his actions. He parked at the far end of the lot where most spaces were empty. He could feel a spring in his step as he felt separated from home and his laptop. The day was fairly cloudy, but he could see the cloud cover starting to break already, which was a great sign for a June day in San Diego. Typically, the cloud cover did not break until early afternoon. Things were looking up.

As Dave opened to door to the store, he could smell the fragrance of coffee and scent of cinnamon in the air. Before he could step in, a woman in a business suit rushed toward the open door with a large coffee in one hand, and a cell phone in the other plastered to her ear, forcing him to step back and let her go by. He thought of a smart response, but only managed a soft "have a nice day" as she dashed to her car without even noticing him. As he stepped into the store, he could not decide if he was upset by her gruff actions, or just jealous that she had somewhere to go. *That used to be me*, he thought to himself.

Three others were in the line ahead of Dave, so he took his place at the end of the line and browsed the menu. He had no need to do so, since he always had exactly the same thing, but it gave him something to do while he waited. Dave was not the type of person to look at other people and listen to their conversations. He was very private in that way. Waiting in line was an uncomfortable position for him, but it was part of life. Soon enough, it was his turn and he moved to the counter.

"Good morning," Bea, the clerk behind the counter said. "Welcome to Starbucks! What can I get for you?"

"I'll have a venti café latte and a cheese Danish," Dave replied. He had seen Bea before, as she had worked there quite some time. Dave had not been there for at least six months, but he remembered her short black pixie-cut hair and bright red lipstick. She was young, probably about twenty-five, and quite pretty. In a way, she looked like Darlene had twenty years ago when they were first married.

"It's Dave, right?" she asked.

"Why yes, you remembered?" Dave stuttered.

"Absolutely," Bea replied as she wrote his name on the cup. "That'll be $5.35, Dave."

Dave reached for his wallet and all the color fell out of his face. No wallet. "Damn it," he said. "My wallet must have slipped out of my pocket in the car. Please just hold that while I go get it. I'm really sorry," he squeaked.

As he turned to leave, the paleness of his face now replaced with red, the man next in line stepped up. "Bea, let me get this one," he told her. "Hey buddy, no sweat, let me get this for you."

Dave turned to face him, with his eyes cast downward. "No, that's okay; my wallet is in the car. It'll only take a moment and besides, I don't even know you," Dave replied.

"The name's Charlie Watson," he said extending his right hand. "I've forgotten my wallet a hundred times; it's really no big deal. Bea, just add his charge to mine. I'll have the usual."

Dave limply shook Charlie's hand, still overcome with embarrassment at the whole incident. Thankfully, Charlie was also the last person in line so Dave did not have a crowd of strangers gawking at him. "Thank you, Charlie."

"You are quite welcome. It's Dave right? That's what Bea called you anyway," Charlie said. "If it makes you feel better, you can buy the next time. I come here all the time, so you can't miss me."

Dave smiled, "That would be perfect, Charlie."

"Great, then why don't you join me now and we can chat if you like," Charlie said motioning to a couple of arm chairs toward the back of the store. After their drinks were ready, the two men moved to the open chairs and sat down.

Dave savored the tart sweetness of the cheese Danish and the richness of the coffee. His color had returned to normal, and the comfort of the chair was already helping him forget the lost wallet incident. He felt great being away from home and the seemingly never ending job search. There really was a world outside his house populated with people other than himself. At times, Dave had begun to imagine that the world was empty with only websites full of offers for jobs that did not really exist, but only keep the unemployed looking and looking without hope. He knew that was not true, but many days it felt that way to his soul.

Charlie Watson was shorter and leaner than Dave. He seemed to be about five feet, eight inches tall, and would be lucky to weigh one hundred and fifty pounds soaking wet. He had short cropped light brown hair and piercing blue-gray eyes. He was wearing sandals, well-worn blue jeans and a black tee-shirt with an odd symbol on the front which Dave had never seen before. His usual turned out to be the same as Dave's, except with a bagel and cream cheese in place of the Danish pastry. Charlie had brought a laptop case with him, but left it on the table unopened.

"So Dave, tell me about yourself," Charlie asked. "I've got all day, so take your time if you like."

There was something about Charlie's demeanor that clicked with Dave. While he told himself to be brief, he launched into a long description of how he was out of work after being with the same company for a dozen years. That company had been acquired by a multinational firm that immediately looked for cost savings measures that ultimately resulted in thousands of layoffs, with Dave among them. He told Charlie how difficult it was to find work these days, and how his mood had been worsening as the weeks went by.

Charlie listened thoughtfully to everything Dave said, nodding in agreement at many of the points. When Dave reached the end, Charlie began, "I know what you are saying Dave. I've been through the same thing, several times. Many companies have become so big that they lose touch with the reason they are in business in the first place. Companies are just communities of people. They exist to make things that help people be happy and healthy, and to provide a living for their employees and share-holders. It is becoming a game among CEOs and others to see who can make the most money." Charlie sipped on his latte, "I don't like what's happening at all. That's why I dropped out altogether!"

Dave was surprised by Charlie's choice of words. "How do you drop out, Charlie?"

"I just found something else to do," he replied. "I have always loved to write, whether it was legal contracts, board presentations, or annual reports. So I figured I could write books or poetry and sell them. It pays the rent now, and I don't need the trappings of business like long hours and countless business trips. Now I can see that I was just wasting my life doing what someone else thought I should do." Charlie finished his coffee with a final slurp to get the last drop. "I come here many days and just listen to what other people are talking about. When I hear something interesting, I open the laptop and start writing about it. It's like the world is doing the writing for me, and all I have to do is add punctuation and send it to the publisher. It's pretty sweet, actually."

"Wow, that's amazing," Dave replied, not certain if he meant it or not. "I'm really sorry for bending your ear for so long, but if it's any consolation, I feel great! Thank you, Charlie. I've got to get going or Darlene will be looking for me." He stood and extended his hand to his new friend, who warmly shook it.

Charlie said, "It was my pleasure Dave. Remember that you owe me a coffee and bagel next time, and then I'll tell you more about me. Have a good day."

Dave picked up his coffee and walked away, happy but confused about the entire morning. It had started out so cold and dismal, but the day looked warm and sunny now, along with his mood. As he walked out the door, he glanced back and saw Charlie opening his laptop.

CHAPTER 2

The following week, Dave had an interview for a job. To celebrate, he and Darlene went to their neighborhood restaurant. They sat quietly together enjoying the food and company. "How did your job interview go, sweetheart?" Darlene asked Dave across the table.

Dave smiled broadly, saying, "I think it went great! Jack, the person I would work for really seemed to like me and my background." He picked up his iced tea glass, clinking it with Darlene's in a toast.

"I really hope it works out for you, babe," she replied. "I know this whole situation has been really hard on both of us. I'm lucky to still have my job; otherwise we'd be in real trouble."

Dave took her hand, caressing it softly. She was right. This had been a difficult time for them. Fortunately, they had ample savings and were able to make ends meet. Their children were grown, so they only had to take care of themselves. Luxuries like vacations were never even mentioned. They still loved to go to restaurants, and allowed themselves to enjoy a bite out when they needed a break, like today. The waitress brought a cup of soup for Dave and salad for Darlene. They sat quietly for a moment, enjoying the food and company.

"Dave, hey, how are you?" Charlie said as he approached their table. "I haven't seen you at the coffee shop recently." He seemed to be wearing the same clothes as the day they met last week. With him was a tall, beautiful woman with a flawless olive complexion and dark brown eyes. Her features were so unique that Dave caught himself staring at her. He had never seen anyone like her, and wondered where she was from.

Dave stood and introduced his wife. Charlie said the woman was his wife, and her name was Aria. They too had stopped for lunch, and seeing him, they just wanted to say hello. After a few minutes, they moved away to their table at the back of the restaurant.

"Wow," Darlene said at last, "that Aria is quite a looker. I noticed you staring at her."

"I've never seen anyone who looks like that. She is definitely gorgeous and so unique," Dave answered. They continued their lunch when the main courses arrived. Dave could see Charlie behind him four or five tables. He was laughing with Aria and teasing the waitress. Dave and Darlene talked about Bill and Cybil, their children, and how Bill just got a promotion and Cybil was pursuing her master's degree while working. Time had flown by with them growing up so fast. Darlene reminded him how they used to fight in the back seat of the car. Dave would be flailing his arm back trying to get them to settle down. They laughed and enjoyed simply being together.

Darlene looked up as two men went by quickly and joined Charlie and Aria at their table. She said, "Those two guys look just like Aria. They have the same complexion and black hair. I wonder if they are related." Dave could see them now.

"They certainly seem a lot like her. I'll have to ask Charlie about that the next time I run into him at the coffee shop," he said. They finished their meal. As they got up to leave, Dave waved goodbye to Charlie. He so was engrossed in the conversation, he did not notice, so Dave and Darlene walked out to their car. As he drove the couple miles back to their home, he thought again about

Charlie, Aria and the other men. Thinking about the three, he could not figure out where they could come from. They looked so different from anyone he had met before. He also thought that he had better go to the coffee shop again soon so that he could repay Charlie's generosity. Mostly though, he thought about the job interview, hoping he would get an offer and put the tortuous unemployment phase of his life behind him.

CHAPTER 3

The next morning, Dave decided he would go to the coffee shop again to repay Charlie. He did not liked owing anyone money, and even the few dollars added to Dave's stress level. It would also give him the chance to find out more about the lovely Aria. Darlene left for work early that day, and so Dave was on his own. After his morning shower and shave, Dave pulled on his clothes and headed out. It was such a beautiful day he decided to walk. The morning air was crisp and cool and the clouds were hung low in the air. The cool breeze felt good on his face. The forecast called for sunshine in the afternoon with a high temperature in the upper seventies, so he knew it was going to be a great day. Dave found himself still surprised by the number of empty houses in his neighborhood. The economy was very difficult, and many of his neighbors had lost their homes to banks and had moved to apartments or even out of the state. He had heard there were more jobs in places like Texas and North Dakota, but Darlene was a San Diego native, with all of her family here, so they stayed.

The walk invigorated him and he could feel a smile on his face. Opening the door to the Starbucks, the same business woman moved toward it, with the cell phone on her ear again. This time, she stopped for a moment, smiled at Dave and thanked him for holding the door. Then she was off to work or wherever she was headed. That small gesture made him smile even more broadly. He was again surprised to see Charlie at the end of the line. The two shook hands warmly and approached the counter when it was their turn.

"Two usuals, guys?" Bea asked. The order was taken, and Dave paid to fulfill his promise. When the drinks were ready, they headed back to the same chairs they had used before. Dave sipped his latte, and smiled contentedly. He felt so comforted by the warmness of the place and his new friend that he forgot his unemployment issue for the moment, instead focusing on Charlie and their conversation.

As promised, Charlie told some of his story this time. After college, he too had gone into the business world, attempting to move up the ladder and achieve financial success. He married Alice, his high school sweetheart and they had two boys together. Charlie focused on his career and moved up quickly, but had to relocate several times in order to take promotions. After fifteen years of moving, the situation became too difficult for Alice and the boys, so they separated and eventually divorced. He kept in close touch with his boys and made certain they graduated from college and had a good start on their own lives. Matt, the eldest, lived in San Diego too, and Charlie loved to visit him and his wife, Elaine, and their young children.

"Charlie, you don't look old enough to be a granddad," Dave said.

"Well Dave, having grandchildren makes you young again. I hope you have that experience soon yourself!" he replied. He continued his story. The next two positions Charlie held were as part of the mergers and acquisitions teams of Fortune 100 companies. He was based in New York City, and traveled seventy-five percent of the time, trying to make the next deal. At the first company, he pulled together a five billion dollar acquisition. After the deal was closed, he was put in charge of the integration process, which included laying-off several hundred employees. That really soured Charlie for this type of business, but it paid very well, and his boys were both in Ivy League colleges at the time. Finally, a somewhat smaller company hired him to run their mergers and acquisitions division.

Chapter 3

That move came with another big raise. He put together half a dozen smaller acquisitions over the first four years. He worked very hard to limit lay-offs and keep an employee-oriented culture. In the fifth year, a very large company acquired them and eliminated Charlie's job, along with several thousand others. That was when he decided to walk away from corporate life and move to San Diego. He spent the first two years decompressing and trying to find a new focus for his life. Ultimately, he began to sit in this Starbucks or other restaurants and just listen to what other people talked about. He realized there were many great stories and he could write about them and maybe publish a book or two.

As Charlie was finishing his tale, the two men who had joined Charlie and Aria at the restaurant entered the store and came to Charlie, who rose and shook their hands. Charlie introduced them to Dave. The taller one was named Muncie Morgan and the other Rence Rialto. Charlie asked them to join them. He then excused himself to buy a couple of coffees for the men.

After an awkward moment of silence, Dave said, "So what do you guys do for a living?"

Muncie replied, "We are scientists, anthropologists, actually." He smiled very slightly, with his large, dark brown eyes glistening. Dave noticed that the two looked like brothers, even down to the long fingers.

"How did you get to know Charlie?" Dave asked.

At that time, Charlie joined them with two cups, which he offered to Muncie and Rence. "That's a great story," Charlie started. "Let me tell you, and guys, please correct me if I've forgotten any details." Charlie told Dave that they had come to him for help in turning their mass of data into a book that would be interesting to non-scientific readers. Too many texts turned out to be very technical, which limited their appeal. Muncie and Rence wanted to get more people interested in anthropology like other scientists had done for astrophysics and quantum mechanics recently. "I think we did a damn good job too, don't you guys?" Charlie finished.

"Absolutely," Rence replied. "But you are forgetting a very important detail, Charlie. There were actually three of us working on this project, and you stole one and married her for yourself. Very selfish of you, my friend."

"Oops," Charlie grinned, "Aria would kill me if I forgot to mention her part is this story. That's why I owe you two so much. If you hadn't come to me, I never would have met the girl of my dreams. Thanks for reminding me, and for having her on your team."

"Charlie," Muncie began, "you are very welcome. But, we do have to get going. We have an important meeting in a little while. Could you come outside with us for a moment? We need to ask you a couple questions." Muncie extended his hand to Dave, "Dave, it's a pleasure to meet you. Have a great day."

"Sure guys. Dave, I've got to get going too. But I'll see you again soon," Charlie finished. The three men left together. Dave could see them hurry around the side of the building. As he sat back, he noticed that Charlie had left his laptop case on the table. He grabbed it and his coffee, and chased after the men.

As he turned the corner of the building, a bright flash of light hit his eyes, forcing him to stop and wince. He reached out with his left hand to steady himself against the side of the building. The brick wall was red hot, and he pulled his hand away letting his coffee cup drop to the ground, spilling its contents on the ground and his shoes. He looked around again and everything seemed normal. He gingerly touched the wall again, and it had cooled substantially and was just slightly warm. Thirty yards or so in front of him, he could see Charlie getting into a dark blue Mercedes sedan. He rushed forward to catch him before he drove away. He was panting for breath when he reached the car.

"Charlie," he gasped, "you forgot your computer bag."

"Thanks Dave," he started. "You saved my life. There are probably ten good book ideas in there. I don't know what I'd do without my electronic brain." He noticed that Dave looked out of breath and somewhat disoriented. "Are you all right, Dave?"

"Did you see that bright flash of light?" Dave asked. "Or did you feel the wall of the Starbucks a minute ago? It was on fire."

"Dave, can I give you a ride home? Please climb in," Charlie said, unlocking the passenger door. Dave got in the car, grateful for the ride as he was feeling a bit dizzy. He told Charlie how to get to his house, and they drove out of the parking lot. "Dave, I want you to know that everything you saw and felt did happen, but please believe me that everything is okay. Even better than that, it's great. I'm not ready to talk about it right now, but I will tell you later. You need to know that this world is a much more amazing and wonderful place than most people could ever imagine. Just keep an open mind and I'll make sure you know everything when the time is right. Okay?"

When Charlie pulled into Dave's driveway, he began again, "Here we are buddy. You should probably just lie down for a few minutes. And maybe put some ice on your hand. It looks pretty red." Dave looked at his left hand and it was quite red, although he did not feel any pain. "Please give me your cell number too, so I can call you later and maybe we can set up another time to talk."

Dave and Charlie exchanged phone numbers. As Dave got out of the car, he almost stumbled. After a second, he felt sure on his feet again. He waved a small goodbye to Charlie, and went inside his house. He took Charlie's advice on the ice and the rest. As soon as his head hit the pillow, he was asleep.

Dave only slept for an hour, but it felt like a full night. He was dreaming about Aria, Rence and Muncie. They were examining him, measuring his skull with a large set of calipers and taking samples of hair and skin. He felt sharp needle jabs in his arms and would see Aria smiling down on him, telling him that all would be okay. She was holding his hand. Her hand felt soft yet slightly cool. Rence was busy writing down the facts and figures. Charlie entered the dream and took the pad from Rence. "It looks like another best seller, team!" he shouted. Dave awoke with a start, his heart racing. His cell phone was ringing in his pocket. "Hello," he spoke almost in a whisper.

"Dave, it's Charlie," he replied. "I just wanted to make sure you were okay. Are you feeling better now?"

"Yeah, thanks Charlie. I think I'm okay now. I'll talk to you later," Dave finished, hanging up. He sat on the side of his bed, the dream fading quickly away. He looked at his left hand, and it seemed normal and back to its usual color. He stood slowly, but felt no dizziness. "Whew, I'm glad that's over," he said walking out of the bedroom.

CHAPTER 4

The following morning, Dave rose early to make breakfast for Darlene before she headed off to work. He could hear her in the shower and hurried to make sure the food would be ready when she was. Dave was a good cook, and had three burners going, the coffee brewing, and bread in the toaster. The frying bacon filled the entire house with its smoky sweet fragrance, fighting for dominance against the freshly brewed coffee. Dave resisted the temptation to pour a cup as he had decided to take his laptop to the coffee shop this morning, like Charlie always did. Perhaps there was special motivation that comes from the blending of coffee and computers. It seemed to work for Charlie.

Dave slipped the over-easy eggs on the plate alongside the bacon just as Darlene entered the kitchen. She kissed him on the cheek and said good morning. He led her to the dinette table and set down her plate. "Thank you, sweetheart," she opened, "What a wonderful surprise! What did you do that I need to forgive?" she laughed.

He laughed. "Nothing dear, just trying to be as sweet to you as you always have been to me." He poured her coffee and added sweetener and milk, just the way she liked it. He grabbed an orange juice from the refrigerator and returned to the table, joining his wife. She sipped the coffee and smiled. Dave sat there for a few minutes; drinking the juice and just watching Darlene eat. They had sat together at that table thousands of times over the years, enjoying meals with the kids, and more recently, the two of them alone. Being empty-nesters was a very different way of life compared to raising Cybil and Bill. There was also so much noise and excitement in the house then. The kids would invite their friends over most days, and they frequently stayed for dinner.

Dave remembered the warmth of family very fondly. Since he had been out of work, he spent most of his days alone in the house, working on his job search and trying to find jobs around the house to occupy his time. The list had become short now after six months, and he had more and more time to sit and think about the difficulty of his situation.

"You must be a million miles away," Darlene interrupted. "It's like you are looking right through me, Dave." She took his hand and squeezed it warmly. "It's okay, sweetheart, everything is going to be fine."

"I was just thinking about when the kids were still here, and they'd invite their friends over in the afternoon," he replied. "Those were just great times. I almost wish I could travel back in time to those days and feel the hustle and excitement again." He held her hand gently, stroking the back of her hand with his thumb.

All too soon, it was time for Darlene to leave for work. Dave walked her to the door and out to her car. As she pulled out of the driveway and down the street, they shared a wave goodbye. He went back into the house, gathered the dishes and put them in the sink to soak as the water warmed up. His mind drifted back to the day he was laid off as he washed the few dishes. He could still feel the pain of losing the job he had held for so long. He talked to several of his former coworkers from time to time. They all told him the same thing; that the company had become completely different since the acquisition. The friendliness of the culture was long gone, and most of the people just worked their eight hours and tried to keep a low profile to avoid the next round of cut-backs. It was so sad, and the pain was still real. Dave was snapped out of his memories by someone ringing the doorbell.

Dave was surprised to find Charlie and Muncie standing at his door, holding a tray of coffees and the small paper bags that Starbucks uses for food items. He welcomed them in and led them to the family room and offered them seats on one of the plush couches. Muncie offered a coffee to Dave, while Charlie took the pastries out of the bags and set the food on top of them.

"I hope you're in the mood for your usual, Dave," Charlie began, handling him a cheese Danish and a napkin. Dave smiled and gladly accepted the pastry.

"Thanks guys. What a surprise. I was planning to take my laptop to the coffee shop today to see if any inspiration hits me like it always does you, Charlie," he replied. Dave sat back into the comfortable sofa and took a long drink of the excellent coffee. Charlie and Muncie exchanged concerned looks.

"Dave, here's the thing," Charlie began. "You saw and felt some strange things yesterday, and Muncie and I are here to answer any questions you may have. There is one caveat to our answering though. What we might tell you is between us. You cannot tell Darlene or any of your other friends and family. At least, not until we tell you that it is okay to tell them. As I said yesterday, there is nothing bad going on, but some folks might think it a bit unusual."

Dave sat up at the edge of the sofa, and looked at Charlie and then Muncie very closely. He checked their eyes for any emotions other than his own anxiety about what he had just heard. He felt none. "Okay, guys, what do we do now?" he said at last.

"Go ahead and ask any question," Muncie replied. "We will answer as best as we can."

Dave thought about the brief time he had known Charlie for a moment. He decided to start with simpler questions rather than jumping to the bright flash and hot wall. "Okay," he began looking at Muncie, "you, Rence and Aria look so different from anyone I've ever seen. Where are you from?"

"Muncie smiled, "I'm from Iowa. I think Rence is from Pennsylvania."

"And Aria is from Washington state, Spokane I believe," Charlie chimed in. "Dave, that's an easy one, but perhaps you didn't state it quite right."

Dave was getting confused, and it showed from the frustration on his face. "What do you mean, Charlie?" he asked.

Charlie turned to Muncie, and said, "When are you from, Muncie?"

Muncie stared directly at Dave, replying, "I was born in the year 3112. I'm not sure about the others, but we're all about the same age. We met while we were in college at MIT. In case you are wondering, I'm seventy-four years old."

Dave's mind was overwhelmed now, and his jaw slackened, leaving his mouth open. He thought this must be some kind of joke. Charlie must be trying to write a new novel about time travel and driving normal people crazy. He cracked a weak smile, saying, "Well, you look damn good for seventy-four. Charlie's a lot younger than you, and he looks like your father."

"Dave, people in my time live much longer," Muncie stated cold as fact. "A few hundred years ago, most people only lived to be forty, and now eighty is pretty commonplace. Time and science keep getting better, you know." He turned to face Charlie. "You know, I'm beginning to think this wasn't such a great idea," he started. "This is a lot for a person to comprehend, especially just being dropped in his lap like this."

"But, we need him, Muncie," Charlie implored. "Dave is a key part of our project, and in order for him to help us, we need to let him know everything. Remember that Rence and Aria were the ones who insisted we add him to our group."

"Rence and Aria insisted on me?" Dave was shocked. He had known these people for less than two weeks. "How or why did they insist on me?"

Muncie and Charlie told Dave the rest of the story. While science, technology and medicine had done marvelous things over the next eleven centuries, it was not a perfect world. Muncie called the period between 1800 and 2200 the Great Period of Integration. Racial and cultural boundaries disappeared. The globe was becoming one giant market and melting pot. That was why the trio from the thirty-second century looked so much alike. Black, Asian, Indian, Caucasian and all other races blended to create the one single race of their time. While a few ethnic enclaves still existed, even they bore little resemblance to their ancestors in 2012.

The Great Period of Integration was followed by two hundred years of warfare, as different governments and cultures fought to dominate the globe. That time was called simply The War, when hundreds of millions of people were killed. New empires formed spanning multiple continents, only to be wiped out by others in a few short years. Much of the scientific gains over the prior millennia were lost in the plumes of nuclear explosions.

The War only ended with the arrival of the first alien species in 2492. That was seen as a great omen, coming exactly one thousand years after Christopher Columbus discovered the New World. The Kalideans had seen the destruction raging for so long that their faith could no longer allow them to sit on the sidelines. Twenty massive battle cruisers came to orbit Earth. They demanded an immediate cessation of all conflict. After all of history, mankind learned for certain that they were not alone in the universe. They finally had a reason to stop hating each other for bits and pieces of land on this lonely rock in space.

Thankfully for the people of Earth, the Kalideans had no desire to be mankind's masters. They began to teach men about the real universe with its countless cultures and civilizations. Their arrival began the greatest scientific and technological era that man had ever seen, and it was continuing in the thirty-second century. In that time, men from Earth had built colonies on five new planets. Earth had trading relationships with hundreds of other worlds. Mankind had grown up, at last.

"Muncie," Charlie began, "you look like you could use a beer. You've been talking for ages. Dave, do you have a couple cold beers for us?" Dave still had his coffee cup in his hand, but it was very cold. He smiled at the men and went to the kitchen to grab the beers. His eye caught the clock on the oven. It read 4:05 PM. He was shocked that so much time had gone by. The whole day had seemed like a dream. He took a beer for himself as well.

"Wow, Muncie," Dave started, "that's unbelievable. Is this some kind of joke? Could any of this be real? I can't believe I never asked about the bright flash and hot wall?"

"Now we're getting to the meat of the story," Charlie shouted. "Let me take it from here Muncie. By the way, you did a great job. Dave, now remember that you can't tell Darlene or anyone else about this right now. You can tell them when the time is right, but not now. Okay?" Dave nodded and took a long drink of the cold beer.

Charlie reminded Dave that Muncie had told him that all things were not perfect in the thirty-second century. Certain diseases could not be eradicated. While people could easily live three or four hundred years, they would likely spend most of their last years wasting away in a hospital. Also, the majority of people were happy to focus on their academics, earning five or more doctorate degrees. Aria had six doctorates herself. Much of mankind's drive to grow and do more had slipped away. Mencius the Kalidean was the representative of their culture on Earth. He served to help mankind reach its potential, and also as ambassador to Earth from Kalidus. He met regularly with the top academics from around the world. A major conference was held in Paris in August 3165 to discuss how to foster the expansion of humanity into the universe. Muncie, Rence and Aria were among the attendees.

Mencius told the group that Kalidus had the same problems five hundred Earth-years before. Their society too had become so homogenous and academic that their growth faltered and the economy almost collapsed. They had lost the spark to innovate and try new things. At the time, the Kalideans occupied fifty planets in their region of space. As growth slowed and society became more timid, five colonies actually failed, with billions of Kalideans forced to move to other planets. The great Kalidean leader of that time, Palidus, convened his best scientific and other leaders to find solutions. At that conference, a young scientist, Mencius, reminded Palidus the Righteous about the rapid growth of their culture when they harnessed dark matter and dark energy to enable time travel. Scientists from their time traveled back to when their culture was only a single planet. They met with the Kalideans who were now known to be their great adventurers, scientists and religious leaders. They mingled with ordinary folks to understand their motivation and what made them different from the Kalideans of Palidus's time. They took the secrets they learned, and some ancient Kalideans back to their time, which then ushered in the Great Expansion, when the Kalidean culture grew from forty-five worlds to over ten thousand.

"So Dave," Charlie finished. "That's about it. That is why Muncie, Rence and Aria came here. Their world needs you, me and some others to help them reinvigorate their society. The bright flash was the time portal closing after Muncie and Rence left Starbucks and returned to their time to make a report. The hot wall was just the after effect of the closing portal. You were dizzy because you have never encountered anything like that before. To tell you the truth, the first five or six times I stepped through a portal, I lost my lunch!"

"More like the first ten times, Charlie," Muncie interrupted. "Whenever Charlie leaps with us, those on the other side know to have a bucket waiting, just in case."

CHAPTER 5

Dave would never forget his first experience traveling through a portal. Stepping through the event horizon was walking into absolute blackness. As his body gradually entered, he felt his body stretched between the dark wormhole and the room he was leaving. Dave could still feel the air in the room on his right leg which had not yet crossed the horizon. The rest of his body was immersed in the absolute darkness, with no sensation of breeze, heat or cold, just black. He could feel the hair on the back of his neck standing up as though he had rubbed his feet on a carpet and was bracing for the zap of static electricity. As his back leg fully crossed the event horizon, Dave felt a momentary stillness and loneliness, as though he was the only person in the entire universe. A light appeared in front of him, growing stronger and larger as it rapidly approached. Dave was very apprehensive and wondered what he could do to avoid being overtaken by it, but he felt suspended in the black without walls or floor or ceiling and couldn't move in any direction. The light resolved into a seven foot circle of light just in front of him. He had been told that this would be the other end of the portal, and he would have to step through it in order to reach his destination. He moved through it, and he felt the warm air and light touching his body and the portal stretching him as though trying to keep him in its sinister embrace. And then, he was out.

Charlie had stepped into the portal just before Dave and was waiting in the room with Muncie and Rence. He smiled broadly, but held a bucket out to him in case his stomach had not made it through yet. "Dave, see, I told you it was easy. By the way, welcome to 3186."

"You know, I lost all perspective on distance and time in that thing," Dave replied. How long did that take?"

"You took one step in, and one step out. How long does that take? One second perhaps?" Charlie said. "The wormhole doesn't exist in the universe. It's just a tunnel between two spots. Since you were momentarily out of the space-time reality, there was no time to be measured. Pretty cool, though? Come on, let's take a look around."

"Where is this place, Muncie?" Dave asked. "Did we travel to another planet or anything like that?"

"Sorry, Dave, we're still in San Diego," Muncie apologized. "We're downtown at City Hall. We're introducing you to some important folks today. I hope you're ready." They exited the room and entered a long hallway. Along one side were windows looking out on the city. The city seemed not that different after eleven hundred years. The buildings were taller, and vehicles seemed to be zipping along both on the streets and in the air above. But it was not like a science fiction movie. Dave was still amazed at how similar all of the people looked. The men all seemed very handsome and the women beautiful, but too similar. They were all quite tall as well. Rence, who was about six feet tall, seemed to be fairly short by their standards. Dave was at least glad to be an inch or two taller than Charlie. The group turned right into a short hall, at the end of which was a sign that read "Office of the Mayor." They opened the door and entered.

The mayor's assistant rose and asked them to sit down while she checked if the group was ready for them. Her name was Lia, and she looked much like the others of this time, except she oddly had blue eyes. She pressed a contact on her headset and waited. Then she stepped to the door and opened it for them. "You may go in now," she said. Charlie walked in just ahead of Dave. Dave thought he heard Lia say "Hi, Dad" to Charlie as he passed. He would have to ask him about that later.

The mayor's conference room was massive. Twenty chairs sat around a thick glass table. One wall was a large window and offered a perfect view of San Diego Bay. On the opposite wall were portraits of previous mayors of the city. Five individuals stood and walked up to them and were introduced to Dave. The first was his host, Mayor Vitek Volomon of San Diego, who warmly shook his hand and welcomed Dave to the future. Next, was Chief Engineer Lanz Lagerfeld, who was responsible for time and space travel. Admiral Arrin Adamsen welcomed him as well. He was charged with the expansion of space exploration and colonization. The final human to be introduced was Bishop Itzak Ibrahim. The Bishop was on the High Council for Humanity which provided leadership for the entire civilization. He would lead the meeting. The last one to be introduced was not human, but not that different either. He was only four and one-half feet tall with bright blue skin. His eyes were black as coal and twice the size of human eyes. His flat nose seemed almost to disappear between those blinking eyes. He wore a long cloak of shimmery, silver fabric.

"Hello Dave, I am Mencius the Kalidean," he began with a low rumble of a voice. "I am very glad that our mutual friend Charlie convinced you to be with us today. It's not that often that we meet our ancestors, or even people from other planets, like me. I can imagine that this is quite a shock."

"Yes, sir," Dave stuttered, "it is an honor to meet all of you."

"Just call me Mencius, Dave," he said and motioned for all to take their places at the table. "We have no need for formalities here. Those are all remnants of the past."

"Mencius," Mayor Vitek broke in. "I will leave you to your guests. I know I am not needed for the meeting. If you require anything, please let Lia know, she is at your disposal." He came up to Dave again and offered his hand. Dave stood and shook it firmly. "Dave, please enjoy your visit to our time. If you are free later, I would love to hear more about this great city in your time." The mayor smiled again and left.

As they sat, Lia and a couple others came in and filled water glasses and placed plates of fruit and cookies around the table. They slipped out as quickly as they had come in.

"Let's cut to the chase then," Admiral Arrin began, "Muncie, why do you need Dave? I mean, he seems like a nice guy, but what does he offer that a general or war hero wouldn't?" He glanced at Dave, saying "No offense to you Dave."

"Frankly Arrin," Muncie began, "we cheated. We know it is against policy, but Rence and Aria jumped ahead a few hundred years and see what happened."

Bishop Itzak jumped to his feet, "This is outrageous! Everyone knows that the future is not set. Any of a trillion minor events now or tomorrow could change it forever. Not only has your team broken every law in the book, but there is no guarantee that what they saw will really happen." Now he stared angrily at Muncie, "How could you let something like this happen?"

"Calm down everyone," Lanz interjected. "It was my idea to jump forward, and I convinced Rence and Aria to do it without telling Muncie until after it was over." Everyone sat again. "We have to remember what made humanity great in the first place. We can't always follow the rules. Sometimes the rules need to be ignored in order for great progress to be made. I sent them separately, and several weeks apart. The results were almost identical in both trips. Sure, some details changed, as the Bishop rightly notes must happen in a living universe. But in my mind, the results were too similar to blame on a minor wrinkle in space-time." He grabbed a cookie and munched at it eagerly.

Charlie had his hand on Dave's shoulder. Dave seemed to be at a tennis match with his head snapping from side to side as the people argued about him. "Okay, I'm game," Charlie said, motioning to Lanz, "what were those results?" There were multiple nodding heads from others to hear the story.

"Rence went first, about two months ago," he began. "He jumped five hundred years and stayed there for about two weeks. He found that humanity has expanded to two thousand planets. There were a number of historical references to David the Conqueror and Brewster the Magnificent. The photographic evidence shows conclusively that Dave here is our man."

"Excuse me," Dave asked, "Are you telling me that I'm some kind of warlord or something? I'm a laid-off accountant from San Diego. Maybe you have the wrong man?"

"Let Lanz finish Dave," Mencius said. "I know this is all very hard to believe, even for me. But let us hear the evidence and we can make a mutual decision on how to proceed." He smiled warmly at Dave, who felt some relief from the call for reason.

"I sent Aria one month later, on two different jumps," said Lanz. "On the first one, I had her arrive two weeks before Rence did on his jump. That was to test if his jump had affected the history he saw. She only stayed two days and focused on history books and videos. She saw the same things Rence would see when he arrived. Then I sent her again for two weeks to a time 800 years ahead of us. Not much had changed about the story. At that time, humanity exists on seven thousand worlds. There was no mention of Dave the Conqueror. The history at that time speaks of David the Wise and Dave the Founder of a Thousand Worlds."

"And the video evidence, Lanz?" Mencius asked. "May we see some of it?"

Lanz pressed a button on the communicator and asked Lia to start the presentation. The window wall turned opaque and a screen opened on one of the smaller walls. Having been advised by his assistant, Mayor Vitek rejoined the meeting to see the present-ation. After a couple of slides specifying the security of the records, it began.

A booming voice filled the room, "In the late 3100s, Mencius the Kalidean helped mankind rekindle the spirit of adventure and exploration. After centuries of stagnation, mankind sought out the best from their past and called Dave the Conqueror, Charlie the Wise and many others to join them and spread humanity throughout the cosmos." A picture of a group of people, along with Mencius, standing on a large balcony came into view. "In this picture we see Dave the Conqueror meeting with the High Council of Humanity to accept the position of High Explorer and Founder of Worlds in 3186." The scene dissolved to a close-up of Dave with Mencius and Itzak on that balcony.

Now Dave really did need that bucket that Charlie had held for him. This had to be a dream. None of this could be true. He wished he was unemployed at home. At least Darlene would be there to hold his hand.

"That video was produced in 3702," Lanz added. The video cards in front of you show the rest of the data we gathered. "Charlie and Dave, our engineers have written the same things onto a DVD that you can look at back home. Please don't let anyone else see this yet. I'm sure you have been advised not to talk about any of this until an appropriate time."

The presentation continued for some time. Dave felt himself spiraling out of control. He was about to be asked to leave his family and life for something totally foreign. He was having a hard enough time taking care of his family now. How could they expect him to fix all of humanity? The announcer said something about the starship Texas leaving on its maiden voyage of exploration, which made Dave look up. There, on the bridge of the ship next to him, holding his hand tightly was Darlene. He could also see Charlie and Aria in the picture. Everyone was smiling. It seemed okay now. He was with the love of his life; and with Darlene around, he knew that everything was going to be fine.

As Charlie and Dave walked back down the hallway toward the portal room, Charlie draped his arm around Dave's shoulders. "Hey, buddy, are you doing all right?" he said. "I know this was a huge surprise for you. Just remember it is your decision. There is no right or wrong or good or bad in the universe. Things just are. If you decide to do this thing, that will be fantastic. If not, that's okay too. The future of the universe isn't written yet. If you stay in 2012, that will be the future. If you come to 3186, that will be the future. You can always go back. It's like your kids, Bill and Cybil right? They moved out of town and now everyone has to travel around to see each other. You can travel to visit them too. Now it's across space and time, but you've already done that once. And you didn't even throw up like me. That makes you twice the man as me already, and you haven't even made up your mind yet. After all, I may become Charlie the Wise, but you could be Dave the Founder of Worlds! That is pretty awesome, friend."

"It certainly sounds amazing," Dave replied. "I don't think of myself as a Founder of Worlds though. Do you think I could do it Charlie?"

"Dave," he said as they turned into the portal room, "what I think doesn't matter. You've already seen evidence that it is true. You saw your own picture and you saw Darlene with you on that ship, ready to face new adventures. You know, I could use a coffee. How about we return to the Starbucks at the same time we left and have a break?"

Dave nodded in agreement. Once the operator initiated the portal, Dave looked around again at the future of San Diego. He could see Mencius walking by, who stopped and waved at Dave before continuing. Dave smiled, and stepped back into absolute black and onto the sidewalk outside the coffee shop.

CHAPTER 6

Dave changed his mind about the coffee and drove home instead. While the first jump did not make him queasy, the meeting and the return jump was too much for him. When he got to the house, he crawled back into bed and thought about what had happened. Did any of that really happen, or was he delusional? He had known Charlie for a couple weeks, and was now being told he would establish new colonies for mankind eleven hundred years in the future. It was just too crazy to take seriously. Dave, the Founder of Worlds; what a joke that was. He knew he was smart and inventive, but still an accountant by trade who rarely traveled beyond his neighborhood. They say each person has a double out there on Earth somewhere. Maybe his double was the real hero of the future. He tried to push any thoughts out of his head. His brain needed time to assimilate this information so he could face the world again. Soon he had drifted off to sleep.

He dreamed of space. He and Darlene were flying through space in a massive ship with thousands of eager settlers milling about. Every other person looked exactly like Muncie. It was a ship of clones. He saw the field of stars in front of the ship, and tried to imagine how many years it would take to reach the first one. The ship started to shake and rattle, and everyone was frightened. It felt like it was about to fall apart. Dave finally woke up to find Darlene shaking him.

"Dave, are you still in bed? It's five o'clock. I just came home from work. Are you okay?" she asked. "You look pale and sweaty." She pulled back the covers. "Jeez, you're completely dressed, shoes and all!"

"Sorry, Darlene," Dave replied, pulling himself up to sit on the side of the bed next to her. "I had a really bad day. I went for coffee with Charlie again, and after that, I felt really nauseated, so I came back home to rest."

Darlene held him close to her, kissing his forehead. "My poor baby, you look a thousand miles away." She helped him to his feet, and they walked into the family room. She helped him sit on the couch, saying, "I'll get us a couple glasses of wine. Then we can both feel better."

Dave was thinking how lucky he was to have Darlene in his life. She was pretty close to being correct: while he was not a thousand miles away, a thousand years away would have been right on the money. He turned on the television to see the news. More bad news about the economy seemed to come out every day. The unemployment rate was up again. No surprise there! Dave knew exactly what that felt like. The news then switched to cover Afghanistan and other global hot spots. More people dying for nothing. He remembered Mencius the Kalidean and his words of wisdom. Perhaps a change of scenery would be good. Maybe he should talk to Charlie and Muncie about the problems in the future. There could be many wars and constant killing there. He had only seen a small part of San Diego. How could he know what else was happening in the future?

Darlene returned with two goblets of red wine, and handed one to Dave. She sat next to him, took the remote from his hand and switched it off. They touched their glasses together and each took a sip of wine. "Ah, that's better," she said, savoring the wine. She reached over and gently kissed his lips. "Dave, I'm afraid I have bad news."

Dave put his arm around her shoulder and pulled her close. "What's wrong, sweetie?" he asked.

"Dave, my company filed for bankruptcy today," she started. "The home office sent everyone an e-mail this morning. Our entire office will be closed in the next four to six weeks." Tears welled in her eyes. "With both of us out of work, I just don't know what we can do. It was such a mess there today. Everyone was freaking out and trying to update their resumes. Oh my God, I'm scared."

Dave kissed her again. "You know Darlene, I know everything is going to be fine," he said. "Charlie and I went to a meeting today about a new joint venture. I'm still not certain if it is right for us, but maybe your loss is a sign that I should take a shot at this."

"Dave, what is the new job about?" she asked. "Tell me more. It would be a miracle if something great came along." She squeezed him tight.

"Sweetheart, it's going to take a few weeks to work on some details. I'm going to call Charlie right now to discuss some of them. The whole thing is a bit shaky right now, so I don't want to get into any details. I don't even know that much yet. But I am beginning to have a good feeling about it. As soon as I know more, I'll let you know too," he finished.

"This calls for a celebration," Darlene beamed, "Let me go get changed and cleaned up, and we can go out to dinner." She rose, then bent over to kiss Dave on the forehead again. Smiling, she went toward their bedroom.

As she walked away, Dave pulled out his cell phone and dialed Charlie. "Charlie, it's Dave. The strangest thing just happened."

"Dave, how are you, pal?" Charlie answered. "You were looking a little stressed after the jump back. Muncie was worried too. Tell me what happened."

"Darlene just lost her job," Dave said. "For some strange reason, I think that's a great coincidence after the meeting we had today. What do you think?"

"Dave, I don't believe in coincidences," Charlie replied. "Everything happens for a reason. This chapter closing for Darlene is a door opening for both of you in the thirty-second century."

"For some crazy reason, I'm beginning to believe the same thing," Dave said. "Do you think we can get together with Muncie or Rence tomorrow to discuss some details that are still unclear to me?"

"No problem. Since it might be a lively discussion, why don't you come to my house? It's more private here," Charlie responded. Charlie gave Dave his address and they agreed to meet the following day. As Dave disconnected the call, Darlene came out of the bedroom looking refreshed and even more beautiful. Dave hugged her close, and the two left for a restaurant, hand in hand.

CHAPTER 7

Dave Brewster had never been in this neighborhood of San Diego before. Charlie was clearly doing quite well. He was driving along past one large gated home after another when he reached a gate in a large stone wall with the address Charlie gave him. As he approached, a tall man in a business suit approached his window. Dave could see that the man had a machine gun slung across his back. The guard was another man from the future with features like Muncie and the rest. He wore a nameplate with "Taron" engraved on it.

"Good morning, Dave," he said. "Charlie and the rest are waiting inside. Please pull to the front entrance and Kally will show you in." Taron touched a button on his belt, and the gate slid open silently. Dave smiled back and pulled through the gate. The driveway was easily two hundred yards long, and a large lawn filled the open space. Rows of annual flowers bloomed along the road side. The house was very big. It looked like one of the mansions in Beverly Hills, with marble columns and a stone façade. As he approached the front of the house, another future-man appeared from the front entrance in a tuxedo. Dave pulled to the side and parked his car. Kally came to the car door and opened it for him. He took the keys and then led Dave through the fifteen foot tall glass front doors and into a large foyer. They walked across the marble floor to a small door to the left of the entrance. Kally opened it and led Dave into the room.

"Dave, I'm glad you found the house," Charlie said as he rose from a couch and crossed the room. They shook hands firmly. "Come on in and have a seat. Muncie had to jump today, but Rence will be down shortly." They walked back to the couch and sat down. "Kally, please bring us some coffee and pastries. Dave, our chef makes the best pastries I've had since I was in Paris." Kally nodded and left the room.

"Charlie, I guessing writing pays pretty well," Dave mused, looking at the beauty of even this small meeting room. The furniture appeared to be antiques, with thick Afghan rugs on the floor and paintings on the walls. Kally reentered the room and set down a tray with a coffee pot, cups, cream and sugar. A woman followed with a tray of pastries, which did look amazingly good. As they were setting everything up, Rence joined them. He came to Dave and shook his hand. Finally, Kally and the woman exited, leaving the three men alone.

"To be frank, Dave," Charlie began, "this place is a front. I've done well with my books, and I had a nice nest-egg when I ended my corporate career, but most of this is paid for by the High Council for Humanity. Almost all of my book income is from sales in the thirty-second century. People of that time love to hear about life in the twenty-first. They are amazed at the diversity and the struggles of existence of our time. Plus, there are a lot more people to sell to. Now, that's progress. Let's have some coffee and relax a bit."

The three men prepared their coffees and helped themselves to the pastries. "Okay, Dave, you have questions, we have answers," Charlie said. "You have me from your time. I am here because I have decided to help our future brothers achieve their destiny. Rence is from the future. He can tell you more about then."

"Rence, please tell me about life in the future," Dave asked. "Is there war and crime? What do people do for a living? What do the Kalideans want from us? I know I'm just rattling off a bunch of thoughts, but I want you to understand that this time is what I know. I am being asked to give it all up for a time I know nothing about." Dave dropped his head for a moment, and then looked into Rence's eyes. "Why should I give up everything I have for you?"

Rence's face flushed bright red. He cleared his throat and adjusted himself uneasily in his chair. "Dave, no one is asking you to give up anything. We believe... I believe that you have an opportunity to fulfill a great destiny in my time. As Mencius told you at the meeting, his society reached a stagnation point, just like mankind in the thirty-second century. They had become so homogeneous that the desire to risk and explore was gone. Just like his people, we decided we needed to go into our past and find those things that have been bred out of us. We needed to rebuild the strength of will we had lost. Otherwise, our society, the society of your future will wither and die. We will become so set in our ways that we will lose all ambition for new adventures and spend all of our lives reading books or traveling through space and time for recreation." Rence rose and walked to the coffee pot for a refill. "If you remember, I have personally traveled to the future of mankind. I have seen the wonderful things we can achieve. I know that you, Dave Brewster, are a key reason for the success of mankind for thousands of years. As a temporal physicist, I also know if you do not take this step, there will be someone else. If you reject us now and forever, I will likely jump ahead again and see what changes have occurred. Of course, there is a chance it will be even better. My experience is that the universe follows the course of least resistance. That is, the flow of the universe and the Will of God follow the shortest, straightest line to the future. Since we hadn't met you yet, and saw that you were in the timeline as a great explorer, I have to believe you are the best choice. What do you think, Charlie?"

"Rence, as always, you answered brilliantly," Charlie beamed. "Dave, please don't feel pressured here. We want you to choose on your own. I want you to know if you go to the thirty-second century, that doesn't mean you can't come here from time to time. You have to commit to making the future your home, but we know your children are here and we don't want them to think you disappeared. You will rent out your house to some of our people. We will take care of everything. When you come back, you can be in your own house. You can visit your children and their children. However, there is one monumental problem you will have to face." As Charlie finished, he walked over to Dave and put his hand on his shoulder. "Dave, if you take this new challenge, you will live probably another two hundred and fifty or three hundred years. Your children will be here in this time, living lives on this time scale. After some time, they will grow old and die, and you will be flying around the galaxy on giant starships full of human colonists. In fact, in every moment when you are in Rence's time, your children will have already been dead for one thousand years."

Tears welled in Dave and Charlie's eyes. Both men knew what they left behind by taking this new calling. "Charlie, how about if I take them with us?" Dave asked.

"Well, that could happen," Charlie answered. "Of course, there are still other family members and friends. We certainly can't take everyone alive now and zip them into the future. If we did, there wouldn't be any generations of mankind to be the ancestors of Rence, Muncie, Aria and the billions of humans alive in the future."

"Dave," Rence started, "You can talk to Darlene now. I want you to know we have the technology to selectively erase certain memories from people. That comes in very handy when we jump. If someone sees a portal open and a person stepping out of thin air, it tends to lead to problems, especially in ancient times like yours. If you two discuss this, and decide not to take this role, I will erase the memories of all of this, except your friendship with Charlie. That way, you and Darlene won't be tortured by the memories or accused of being insane by your families and neighbors."

"Thanks, Rence, I guess that's good to know," Dave replied, shifting uneasily in his chair. "So, I go home now and talk to Darlene? She'll be the one who thinks I'm insane. Being out of work has halfway driven me there already."

"Dave, how about if Aria and I invite you two to dinner here tonight?" Charlie asked. "That way, you will have us to show her that it is all true. Rence, perhaps you could get permission for all of us to jump and meet with some folks, and see some sights. All Dave has seen so far is the mayor's office in San Diego. Perhaps Dave and Darlene should have a grand tour."

"That's a great idea, Charlie," Rence said. "Rather than me talking about the future, let's have Dave and Darlene live there for a while. Dave, you know we can jump out and back in the same minute, but spend as long as we want in the future, right?"

"I honestly hadn't thought about that, Rence," Dave smiled. All of them laughed. "Okay, Charlie, call me when it's all set up and tell me when to bring Darlene over."

"If not tonight, tomorrow for sure," Charlie replied. The three rose, shook hands, and Dave walked out the door. As Dave reached his car, Charlie called out, "One last thing, Dave. You can tell Darlene that I hired you today on a temporary basis. I need you to research my new book on time travel. I'm paying $10,000 per month, okay? Don't worry, Lanz and Mencius already approved it."

"You never fail to amaze me, Charlie. I accept!" Dave said as he climbed into his car. As he headed home, his mind was on fire. "Living in the future and being a great explorer; could any of that be possible?" he thought to himself. It seemed impossible to be true. He had no idea how Darlene would respond to these revelations. Dave could barely handle it himself. "As long as Darlene and I are together, everything will be okay," he thought as he pulled onto the freeway.

CHAPTER 8

The following evening, Dave and Darlene were driving back to Charlie's house. The sun was sliding down toward the horizon, and the temperature was starting to drop from the high of eighty degrees. Darlene had been happy with the news about the job, but apprehensive about whether it was real or would last. Dave had known Charlie a couple of weeks, but now he was going to pay him $120,000 a year to help write a book? It seemed too good to be true. How could a casual friendship developed at a coffee shop turn into such a great job so quickly? As Dave turned onto Charlie's street, her fears dropped a bit when she saw the massive homes that lined the street. "Wow, Dave, Charlie does live in a nice neighborhood," she gasped as each house seemed larger than the one before. As Dave turned into Charlie's driveway, Taron was there again, smiling broadly.

"Dave, it is good to see you again," Taron began. "This must be Darlene," he said reaching through the window to shake her hand. "It's a pleasure to meet you. My name is Taron. Charlie and Aria are waiting for you both inside. Dave, you know the drill. Kally will take you inside." Taron touched his belt and the gate slid open easily.

"Thanks, Taron," Dave said, as he pulled ahead through the gate and up the driveway. "Nice place, right Darlene?"

"It's unbelievable Dave. I've never seen such a beautiful house before," Darlene replied as she squeezed his hand. "I noticed the guard looks a lot like Aria and the others. Did you ever find out where they were from, sweetheart?"

"Yes, but I think I'll let them explain it all. It was a bit complicated," he said as they approached the front of the house. Kally was already out the door and approaching them. Kally opened Darlene's door and offered his hand to help her out. She thanked him, and he hurried over to Dave's side. Dave handed him the keys, and the group headed toward the front doors. Charlie was waiting at the door. He kissed Darlene on the cheek and shook Dave's hand heartily.

"I'm so glad you two were able to come this evening. Follow me over this way. The rest of our guests are waiting for us through there," Charlie said. They crossed the room to an open door and stepped in. They were in a small room with a large computer panel, and Dave immediately recognized it as the portal unit. Rence was standing behind the control panel, quickly typing instructions on the keyboard. "Darlene," Charlie started, "I don't know if you remember seeing Rence that day at the restaurant with Aria and me?"

"Hello, Darlene," Rence said. "We've very glad you could come." He continued tapping on the keyboard.

"Dave," Darlene asked apprehensively, "What is going on here? What is this place?" She held his hand tightly.

"Dave, let me handle this one." Charlie continued, "Darlene, we are going to join Aria for dinner now. There is nothing to be afraid of. Rence, please signal Aria to join us here." Rence keyed a new command on the panel. On the far wall of the room, a small black circle began to appear and grow. Within a few seconds, it had grown to seven feet in diameter. It was absolutely black with no sound or heat or any other sensation, only blackness. A leg appeared in the black circle, and almost immediately the rest of Aria stepped into the room from the black circle. Dave could feel

Darlene's legs buckle a bit and he put his arm around her waist to support her.

Aria stepped forward and kissed Charlie lightly on the cheek. "Is everything okay here sweetheart?" she asked him. Seeing Darlene and Dave, she moved to them and said hello, kissing each on the cheek.

"Darlene doesn't know anything about what's going on yet, you know," Charlie said. "This must be quite a shock to you. Aria and I wanted to take you somewhere special for our first dinner together. That place is just through there," he finished pointing to the black circle on the wall. We're going to be late for our reservation, so let's go." Charlie took Aria by the hand and the two stepped into the black circle, and were gone.

Darlene looked pensively at Dave. "Honey, I know none of this makes sense, but we need to follow them. Everything is going to be okay, and we'll be together the whole time," Dave said, trying to calm her nerves enough to make that first step. "Take my hand; this is going to be fun." He turned to Rence, "Hey, are you coming too?"

"I'll be right behind you two," he replied.

Darlene took Dave's hand and smiled at him. They stepped toward the black circle. Dave could feel the fear in her and rubbed her back a bit to calm her. They stepped into the circle and were gone. Rence set the automatic shut-off, and hurried around the counter and stepped into blackness. A few seconds after he stepped in, a blinding flash filled the portal room, and the black circle was gone.

Dave and Darlene stood in absolutely blackness. She tried to speak to him but he could not hear her words. Soon, a white dot formed in front of them, growing quickly to a seven foot circle. They could hear sounds from the white circle and thought they could even smell food. Dave took her hand more tightly and motioned her to step through the circle with him. They stepped through the circle and into a restaurant halfway up the Eiffel Tower.

Charlie stood there smiling, holding two white buckets, just in case. Aria stepped forward and handed each of them a flute of champagne. "Welcome to Paris you two!" she giggled. Everyone enjoyed a sip of champagne. Dave and Darlene were led to their seats, which had a magnificent view of the city rising along the Seine. The nearby Arc de Triomphe was shining under the lights as vehicles zipped along and above the Champs-Elysees. The Brewsters had always dreamed to traveling to Paris after they retired. They never had the money to take a family vacation to such a place. Now, here they were. But it looked so different from the pictures and television programs they had seen.

"Dave," Darlene whispered in his ear, "are we really here? Ten seconds ago we were in San Diego, and now Paris. How is that possible? What about the nine hour time difference? Shouldn't it be six in the morning in Paris now? Also, everyone here has the same features as Aria and the rest. What's going on?"

Charlie stood up and turned to Dave and Darlene, saying "Darlene, I know you have a million questions going through your head right now. And while we enjoy a fabulous dinner, we are going to explain everything. We have two special guests joining us who will help explain everything." The two men had been sitting at the table, but Dave was too preoccupied with Darlene to have noticed them. Chief Engineer Lanz and Bishop Itzak rose and stepped over to Darlene to welcome her.

Chapter 8

Course after course of dishes were brought to the table. Champagne and wine flowed freely. Dave was thankful that at least these decadent pleasures from the twenty-first century had not been lost. Darlene hovered between the joy of the location, the food and Dave's nearness, and the fear and doubt about what was being said. Itzak led the discussion while Lanz focused on the technological aspects of their journey through space and time.

The narratives were the same that Dave had heard at the San Diego mayor's office. Dave was destined to found many new colonies for humanity. Darlene the Benevolent was recorded in history as well, as she helped bring many races of the universe together to enable friendly expansion of each. Itzak noted a specific example of the Galliceans. They were a race that thrived on gas giant planets, occupying three thousand worlds near both the Kalidean and human spheres of influence. Ambassador Darlene Brewster negotiated a treaty exchanging access to earthlike planets in Gallicean systems for gas giants in human star systems. That enabled all of them to have access to more planets while sharing resources and building their bonds of friendship.

As the waiters cleared the table to serve dessert, Darlene broke in, "This is an incredible story. Thank you for taking your time. Now, I am a simple woman from your past, and I have a few simple questions." They nodded politely for her to continue. "First, what happens to our family in our time? Would we ever see them again?"

"Darlene," Charlie said, "Please let me answer that one since I have personal experience with this. "As Dave knows, I have two boys in the twenty-first century, Matt and Robert. I worked out a deal where I can visit my family from time to time. Recently, I've been spending a lot more time in the twenty-first, while I've been recruiting you two. Normally, I spend a year in the thirty-second and then I jump to the twenty-first for a one week visit." Darlene frowned. "But, you have to understand time travel, Darlene. After that one year, I jump back to just a week or two after I left. To my family, it hardly seems like I've been gone at all."

"But how can you do that? Can't they tell by your age?" she asked. A week later you look a year older. That doesn't make any sense."

"Darlene," Aria started. "We weren't at that point yet, but people in our time live between three and four hundred years." When Charlie joined us in the thirty-second, he was given the same immunizations and vaccinations that we all receive. With his strong metabolism and drive from his time, he'll probably outlive us all!"

"Darlene," Itzak said, "You and Dave would be a great asset for us in our time. As we've told you tonight, our future history will be greatly improved and humanity will thrive for thousands of years in the galaxy if you join us. It would be foolhardy for us not to protect such great people. How many planets can you colonize or how many peace and trade treaties can you negotiate if you live only another thirty or forty years?"

"Plus your work is not yet complete in the twenty-first," Lanz said. "There are the others to be considered, Itzak."

"Yes, I know. I am not certain that tonight is the time to speak of this, but since you brought it up, and I am a member of the High Council for Humanity, let's show all of our cards," Itzak replied. "Aria, please share what you have learned of our future." Charlie, Muncie and Rence looked very surprised. Clearly, this was information that they had not yet been told.

Aria cleared her throat, looking first at Charlie, holding his hand and then at Dave and Darlene. "When I jumped to the fortieth, I found that there had been a major change in human lifespan. People there lived as much as one thousand years. That is on a scale equivalent to the Kalideans or Galliceans. Apparently, the major shift occurred in the thirty-third. A team of scientists who received multiple medical and scientific degrees in the thirty-second and thirty-third had uncovered methods to perfect DNA performance, leading to the longer lives. When I researched the team, I found they were from the twenty-first as well as thirty-second centuries." Aria took a long drink from the Badoit water on the table. "The team member names recorded were William Brewster, Cybil Brewster, Matthew Watson, and Robert Watson from the twenty-first century, and Lia Lawson, Rence Rialto, and Jake Maklan from the thirty-second." She sat heavily in her chair.

"Wow," Rence, Charlie, Dave and Darlene said almost in unison.

CHAPTER 9

After returning home, Darlene had a difficult time trying to sleep. The portal had been adjusted to return them at 10:00 PM on the same day they left, just as though they had gone to a dinner in town. Dave kept asking her what she thought about all of this during the drive home, but Darlene was lost in her thoughts. She never heard him say a word. When they arrived at home, she changed into her pajamas quickly, kissed Dave on the cheek and went right to bed. Sleep did not come easily. She tossed and turned with thoughts of the future flashing through her mind. Everything she had ever known was now out the window, and these strange people from the future were asking them to pack up and live in their world. As a wife and mother, Darlene had her share of sleepless nights, and had learned to push all thoughts from her mind. Then she would consciously force her mind to stay empty and quiet. After a few minutes, she fell asleep.

Dave was too overwhelmed with Aria's admission to even try to sleep. He put on his pajamas and went to the family room to relax, giving his wife some privacy with her thoughts. He poured some whiskey over ice and sat on the couch with his feet up on a hassock. He took a sip and sighed heavily. His cell phone rang. "Hello?"

"Dave, it's Charlie," he began. "Darlene looked pretty dazed when you left us. Is she okay now?"

"She'll be fine, Charlie," Dave answered. "That information from Aria was shocking to all of us, in a good way. Did you know any of this about your own children?"

After a moment, Charlie replied, "No, no I didn't. I was thrilled in one way, but a bit hurt that Aria hadn't told me before." There was a moment of silence, and he began again, "You have to understand the time travelers from the future, Dave. Only a handful of people are allowed to jump in time. The risk of contaminating the past or future with unforeseen changes is too great. I think I heard that there are only ten or twenty official jumpers in the thirty-first. That includes those of us who have been given special privileges since we have given up so much by abandoning our own time."

"I guess that makes sense, Charlie," Dave said. "All the science fiction I've ever read was full of warnings about time travel. What was that old paradox? Oh yeah, what would happen if I traveled back in time and killed my father before I was conceived? How could I exist in the future to travel if I had never been born? Something like that."

"Lanz and Aria tell me that the universe is a lot more resilient than we think," Charlie commented. "God, the universe and space-time take care of those things by not allowing them to work. Somehow. I don't know, it's way over my head. I'm just glad that Darlene is okay, and I hope she can get some rest. If you're up for it, I'll meet you for coffee at Starbucks tomorrow, okay?"

"I'll try to be there. It depends on how Darlene feels after she has digested that fabulous French dinner and the revelation of being Darlene the Benevolent. Good night, Charlie, and thank you for being my friend. And for giving me a job," Dave finished.

"Dave, by now you should have realized that the High Council for Humanity is your real employer. I'm happy to know you too, pal. Have a good night," Charlie said, and broke the connection. Dave put his feet up to feel more relaxed, sipping his drink and imagining what would happen in the morning and how it would feel to be Dave the Founder of a Thousand Worlds. He finished his drink and went to bed.

Darlene had a difficult night. She dreamed about flying through space with a ship full of those unusual looking future humans. She dreamed of meeting the Galliceans, who appeared to be blobs of gas with a thin skin. She saw Bill and Cybil in the future working in lab coats on extending human life. Bill came to her with a giant needle, easily three feet long, and told her that it would not hurt as he jammed it into her chest. She shot up straight in bed, drenched in sweat and breathing heavily. Dave was sound asleep next to her. It had only been a dream. She relaxed quickly and lay down next to Dave, caressing his face with her fingertips. She was about to drift off to sleep when a brilliant flash appeared in the living room, and she was frightened again. Was she still asleep? She did not think so, but was too afraid to investigate the flash.

She heard Aria's voice saying softly, "Darlene, it's Aria. I'm sorry to scare you like this, but there is someone I want you to meet. Please come out here, but don't wake up Dave, okay?" Darlene composed herself and pulled on a robe, and walked into the living room, with no idea what to expect.

Cybil was standing there with Aria. Darlene ran to her and hugged her close. "My baby, it is so good to see you. What are you doing here, and how do you know Aria?" she asked. She turned to Aria, "What's going on, Aria?"

"Mom, let's go into the kitchen. I don't want the light to wake up Daddy," Cybil said. The three walked into the kitchen and Cybil switched on the lights. Darlene knew now that something terrible had happened. Cybil's face had aged and her hair was turning gray. Aria also looked much older. Darlene touched Cybil's face and tears welled in her eyes. Cybil took her mother into her arms and hugged her.

"What's happened to you Cybil? You look so different. Did the time travel do this to you?" Darlene asked, crying now.

"No, Mom," Cybil began, almost giggling. "I'm four hundred and fifty years old. Look at poor Aria, she's over five hundred now. We thought it might be good to come here now and let you know that everything will be okay. Bill and I are still working together, even though the DNA project is finished."

"Darlene," Aria began, "we can only stay a few minutes. It took me a long time to get approval for Cybil to jump, even this one time. We will both be in a lot of trouble if we don't get back to the thirty-fifth pretty soon. I want you to know your children are doing fine in the future, but it is still your choice whether to stay here or come with Charlie and me. Time is very resilient, and things will always happen according to the flow of the universe and God's Will. Cybil, we need to go now." As they turned to return to the portal, they saw Dave standing in the door crying.

Dave hugged his daughter and kissed her on the cheek. "My little girl, all grown up. Will I ever see this?" he asked.

"Daddy, you and Mom are still with us in my present," Cybil said stroking his hair, "although you don't have this much hair anymore." She kissed him on the cheek. "We've got to go, but we'll have our full lives together, here or in the future. I love you both." Aria and Cybil walked into the living room and into the open portal. A flash of light lit the room, and then went dark. Dave and Darlene hugged, and walked back to the bedroom, warmed greatly by such a wonderful surprise.

CHAPTER 10

Dave Brewster could still remember the first time he met Charlie Watson. It has been several months now, but the events of that day were stuck in his mind forever. Dave sat quietly sipping his cappuccino in the lounge of the star cruiser Reliant. He took a bite of the luxurious chocolate croissant. Charlie had introduced that treat to Dave recently, and he had happily switched from cheese Danish. The dark chocolate worked so well with the flavor of hot coffee. He felt very relaxed, and looked about the coffee shop, watching other people enjoying their break or breakfast at the beginning of their day.

"There's Dave the Explorer," Charlie said as he entered the room and walked over the Dave.

"Charlie, you know I am not comfortable with that name," Dave replied. Charlie sat down next to him and took a sip of his drink. They both felt very relaxed to share this time together.

A beep sounded in Dave's earpiece and he touched it lightly, "Yes, Captain, what's up?"

"Admiral," started Cadiz Carlyle, Captain of the Star Cruiser Reliant, "twenty minutes ago a Gallicean starship jumped through the Io Space Portal and has assumed an orbit over Jupiter. Our Ambassador has jumped from that ship to Reliant. She is now refreshing herself in your quarters. Darlene has asked that we meet with her in your ready room in fifteen minutes."

"Very good news, Cadiz, thank you," Dave finished and cut the connection. Darlene had been gone for three weeks with High Commissioner Darak Daniels and Mencius the Kalidean on a mission to develop a treaty for sharing star systems with the Galliceans. It was a very good sign that a Gallicean starship had jumped to our solar system. Orbiting Jupiter was another good sign, as that would be an ideal planet to offer them for colonization. "Charlie, good news about Darlene's trip," he said. "She's back here now and we're meeting in fifteen minutes in my ready room to discuss. You'll be there, of course?"

"I wouldn't miss it for the world," he replied. "It's about time that we started on this adventure. Let me go get better dressed and I'll meet you there." Charlie hurried out of the room. After Dave finished his coffee, he walked over to the large viewing port in the coffee shop and looked out on the Space Dock where the three large colonizing ships were being completed and prepared. The Ticonderoga was his flagship and was already completed. It was currently being fueled and stocked for its first mission. The Berlin and California would be completed within a month. Each ship was massive, at one thousand meters long and four hundred meters across. Ten thousand settlers and crew would live on board for months as they traveled to and terraformed new colonies. The crescent of Earth filled half the view as sunrise was just coming to North America. Dave could see several dozen ships orbiting Earth, including four other star cruisers like the Reliant.

The beep sounded in his ear again. He again recognized the tone as Captain Cadiz. "Yes, Cadiz, what is there to report?"

"Dave, the Colony at Day's End has asked us to send ships there to defend against pirate activity in their zone," Cadiz reported. "Apparently, the few remaining colonists from Far Sky colony have resorted to piracy to maintain themselves. I suggest we sent Defiant and Courage as soon as possible."

"I agree, Cadiz. Please work with their captains and HQ to get them on their way. Ask HQ to give them priority for fueling over the colony ships." Dave replied as he closed the connection. Far Sky colony was one of the details that had been conveniently left out of the briefings that Dave and the other twenty-first trans-plants received prior to their acceptance of this new life. As with the Kalideans, humanity had two colonies that failed when society had begun to stagnate.

Those colonies, Far Sky and New Dawn were the last ones established before humanity began to lose its desire to stretch and grow. Each was home to hundreds of thousands of immigrants who were beginning to build factories and economies to support themselves and the rest of mankind. As people lost the desire to explore and expand, supply shipments slowed and eventually stopped. Most settlers returned to Earth and the established colonies. Some became so disenchanted with the rest of society that they decided to remain and forge independent lives. New Dawn was virtually deserted, and Earth lost contact with the few residents quickly, none of whom had been heard from in hundreds of years. The population of Far Sky dropped from six hundred thousand to just over one hundred thousand during the exodus back to the settled planets. Most of the residents led simple agrarian lives, and were content to let their colony grow naturally over time. Without resupply or factories and institutions of their own, health care and safety began to suffer after the first one hundred years. Life spans dropped from the normal three hundred and fifty to a low as one hundred years without the advanced medicines so readily available on the settled planets. A few years ago, Kalidus sent an expedition there to learn about the situation of the people. The Skyers, as the residents were called, seized the ship and its supplies. The Kalidean crew was lucky to escape using a portable portal they carried with them. With the new ship in their arsenal, the Skyers are beginning to raid other colonies to get what they wanted. Day's End was the closest established colony and took the brunt of the attacks. Fortunately for all mankind, the portals on board the Kalidean ship were disabled by the crew when they fled.

Life in the thirty-second was not as ideal as Dave and Charlie had been led to believe. But that was a matter for Arrin and his star fleet to manage. Dave's team needed to focus on the Galliceans.

CHAPTER 11

Dave hurried to the ready room to be there before the others arrived. As the door opened, he saw Darlene standing at the end of the conference table smiling widely at him. He rushed to her and kissed and hugged her to him. "Welcome home, sweetheart," he said with tears welling in his eyes.

"It's good to be back with you," she replied, wiping the moisture from his eyes. "You can't imagine how great it is not to have to wear a pressure suit all day and night!" The door opened and the rest of the staff entered and exchanged greetings with Ambassador Brewster.

As they sat to listen to Darlene's report, the voice of Communications Officer Lia Lawson came over the speaker, "Admiral, we have an incoming message from the Gallicean ship, Kong-Fa. It is their captain, De-o-Nu who wishes to speak to you," she said.

"Put it in here, Lia, and make certain the captain knows all the folks he is speaking to," Dave replied. Lia sent the communication through the translator to them.

"Greeting, Admiral Dave Brewster. I am De-o-Nu, Captain of the glorious Star Ship Kong-Fa. I have the honor of hosting our great General Fa-a-Di, who has come here to thank all humanity for the negotiations recently held on Gallia, and to personally scout the gas planets that you have offered to us," the voice said.

"Dave," Darlene began, "this is big. General Fa-a-Di is the current leader of the Gallicean High Council. This probably means the treaty will be accepted. I wasn't told he was on board during the trip here."

Dave nodded to her, pressed the com-link and replied to the Gallicean, "Captain De-o-Nu, it is a tremendous honor for us to host the General, you and your crew in our solar system. You know that our Ambassador Brewster is here with us today?"

"Yes Admiral, I was so advised. Ambassador, it is an honor to speak with you again. I hope you enjoyed the hospitality of my crew on our voyage from Gallia?" he replied.

"Captain De-o-Nu," Darlene began, "your crew members were wonderful hosts, and we all look forward to meeting with you on Io. Please let us know your schedule, and we will be there."

"Thank you Ambassador," De-o-Nu replied. "The general has requested a two Earth day resting period before our meeting. We are launching probes to all four gas planets so that we can analyze their suitability to us. The physical needs of Galliceans are unique, as are the needs of all species. I'm certain you understand that. That being said, the general has told us he is confident we will agree on the treaty whether or not these particular planets are suitable."

"That is great news," Dave said. "We will leave shortly to begin our voyage and arrive at the appropriate time. I also want you to know we are building a site on Io that will accommodate both humans and Galliceans. It may not be ready soon, but as our relationship grows, we will need this and many other such sites so our peoples can learn to work and live together."

De-o-Nu laughed. The translator could not translate laughter, so the people in Dave's meeting heard a high pitched squeal. Darlene told them the sound was indeed Gallicean laughter. "Your people are as generous as we have been told by our great mutual friend, Mencius the Kalidean. I will pass along your kind words to the general and we will await your arrival here.

Admiral, just so you know, Mencius and Darlene have told us many things about you and your friend Charlie. The general and I are very much looking forward to meeting you both. Kong-Fa out." The line went dead.

Everyone around the table was smiling. The mission to expand humanity had begun. In the back of Dave's mind, he was still thinking about the lost colonies of Far Sky and New Dawn. Somehow he would have to make those places a priority, and reestablish those colonies. They had been chosen in the first place, and it was not fair to the brave settlers to be lost in the dust of history. He knew the piracy was an act of desperation by people who had been lost and forgotten by their brothers and sisters. That could not stand. Before humanity could truly begin to grow, it must face up to its failures and bring those souls back into the fold. That was why the Kalideans had intervened in The War. Their beliefs could not let them watch as others suffered and died out of arrogance or stupidity. Dave could not allow those settlers to suffer because they had been forgotten by their home world.

The communicator cackled again, and Lia's voice said, "Dave, High Commission Darak has jumped on board. He would like to meet with Darlene as soon as possible." Darlene excused herself and walked out.

Dave replied, "Lia, let them have Captain Cadiz's ready room please. I'm going to keep the Captain here for a while."

The meeting continued for another hour. Dave asked the crew to prepare to leave within two hours with a course to arrive at Io in two days. Individuals left when they understood their assignments until only Cadiz and Charlie were left. "I have a special project for you two," Dave started. "One of our first priorities needs to be fixing the situations at Far Sky and New Dawn. No one knows if anyone is still alive on New Dawn. We do know that there are pirates on Far Sky. Cadiz is arranging for two cruisers to head to Day's End immediately to scout the situation. I don't know how it can be done, but I need you two to come up with ideas on how we can rebuild those colonies first. It's not fair to the people there that they were deserted by us. It's no wonder they have to resort to piracy to get food and medicine. Desperate people do desperate things."

"Wow," Charlie replied. "That's a big order, Admiral. I think you are right on this, but it isn't going to be easy."

"No easier than terraforming a new planet," Cadiz jumped in. "And certainly no easier than scouring a million solar systems for habitable planets. Admiral, if you don't mind, I'd like to ask Arrin for help or other contacts that can help us here."

"That's a great idea, Cadiz! Thank both of you for this help," Dave replied, comforted to have help in this quest.

"Do you think Charlie and I should go to Day's End with the other cruisers now?" Cadiz asked.

"No, not just yet," Dave answered. "First, I want to get an idea of how bad the piracy situation is. Second, we really need to expand our network and get more people to help with this. Maybe you can find relatives of people who left or stayed on those planets and get their advice. But you also heard De-o-Nu. He is very interested in meeting Charlie. I wouldn't want to deprive him of that pleasure." They all laughed and left the room together.

CHAPTER 12

Dave and Charlie stood on the platform suspended in the Jovian atmosphere. Although they had eagerly agreed to this, they could not help but feel very apprehensive. Humans and Galliceans were just beginning to form a relationship, and now they were putting their lives in the hands of General Fa-a-Di and Captain De-o-Nu. Darlene had told Dave that this was a great honor to explore Jupiter with the general, but here, trapped in the pressure suit with a limited air supply deep inside the massive gas ball did not seem so honorable. Neither man had ever seen a Gallicean in their natural element. On Io, they had to wear pressure suits to survive in the earthlike structures built there. They had been impressive in those suits. Each one was more than ten feet tall, and their bodies seemed mashed to fit into the confines of the suits. These were creatures who lived on gas giant planets with no habitable surfaces. How they had come to build a civilization of thousands of planets? They had so many questions for the general.

As they pondered these questions, a Gallicean shuttle pulled up to the platform, and the door silently opened. Dave had seen Gallicean faces through the cloudy masks of their pressure suits, but their features were not at all clear. Now Dave was in their element and was the one with unclear features behind the heavy glass of his mask. When the first stepped out, Dave was awestruck. The creature was easily fifteen feet tall as it stretched out on the platform, unfurling wings that seemed to be thirty or forty feet across. The face was birdlike, with large, unblinking black eyes and a hawk-like beak for a mouth. There were no feathers, but a shiny, almost iridescent skin. The rest of the body was lean, apparently to lessen the weight to keep it aloft. It approached Dave and stretched out a surprisingly human-like hand, which Dave shook.

A thunderous squeal of laughter filled Dave's ears, as his translator sprang to life in his ear. "Admiral Dave," said Fa-a-Di as he shook his hand, "it is wonderful to be here with you today. I think you will enjoy this a great deal." As he spoke, a second Gallicean left the shuttle. The second was even larger than the general. He seemed to be twenty feet tall with an even larger wingspan. "De-o-Nu, are you ready to show our friends a good time?" the general said as he slapped the captain on the back.

"General," he began, "I've been looking forward to this a very long time. Exploring a new planet for the first time is a thrill for me. Normally, I am the one who must stay on board and manage the ship. Thank you for the opportunity."

"De-o-Nu, since you married my sister, I know I have to take better care of you," he laughed. He turned his attention to Dave and Charlie. "Gentlemen, today we are going to take a short visit to Jupiter and look for anything that seems unusual. The reports from the probes have shown that both Jupiter and Saturn are great planets for us and it is our custom to search for things the probes might have missed. De-o-Nu and I are wearing a special harness to carry you with us. I will carry Dave. All four of us will be able to communicate through our com-links. I asked your crew to attach as special device to your suits so that if you become detached from us, it will return you to the platform. No one wants an interstellar crisis if one of you drops to the surface and is crushed by the gravity. We will be going quite deep in the atmosphere to measure the depth of the habitable band. Your crew put a special device in the glove of your left hand. If the pressure becomes uncomfortable, clench your fist and we will return here as well. Are you ready to begin?"

Dave and Charlie were too overwhelmed to utter a word, but nodded their heads to let them know they were ready. Two more Galliceans joined them on the platform. They hoisted Dave into

Chapter 12

Fa-a-Di's harness, and Charlie into De-o-Nu's. After securing the humans, checking their air supplies and pressure levels, they saluted the general and captain and returned to the shuttle. "Enjoy the ride, dear friends," said the general, who then laughed again, the loudest they had ever heard. The Galliceans dived over the edge of the platform into the Jovian atmosphere.

They dove for what seemed like minutes to Dave, who was dazed by the swirling walls of gas they flew through. Fa-a-Di's body seemed bloated with the gas as if he was consuming it. After a second, Dave realized this was a new, fragrant atmosphere for the general and he was probably enjoying the fresh air. "Dave, we will be traveling through several bands of clouds that are moving in opposite directions. It might be a bit bumpy, but don't worry, you will be fine," the general said. "Brother-in-law, the air is so fresh and clean here," he continued, "nothing like on Gallia or any of the other high population planets."

"You are right, Brother, it is like a fresh spring day after the rains," the captain replied. Dave turned to look at the captain and Charlie and saw De-o-Nu unfurl his wings to a full fifty foot span, which slowed him down so quickly that Dave lost sight of him in the clouds swirling above him.

Fa-a-Di opened his wings and Dave could feel them leveling off and slowing down. That was a relief. Dave was imagining himself crushed against the general by the massive pressure further below. Ahead, Dave could see a wall of greenish clouds moving incredibly fast across their path. He braced for impact. "Hang on tight, Dave," the general said as they slammed into the clouds.

The two tumbled about for a few seconds before the general could regain control. He laughed out loud, and Dave thought he could see a smile on his beak. "Quite a ride, general!" he gasped.

"Wow!" Fa-a-Di shouted. "This really is a wild world you want to give us Dave. All the development on our home worlds has destroyed much of the thrill of a gas planet. It has been many years since I've had that much fun. Brother, did you see the green band of gas?"

"I'm headed that way now, Brother," De-o-Nu said. "Tell me about it."

"The air is even better here, but brace for the impact. The winds are very strong. Hold on a minute, I see something interesting. Get over here now, Brother, we have an adventure afoot," the general finished. The captain arrived within a minute to where the general was hovering. "Brother, look down there," Fa-a-Di said, pointing lower in the atmosphere.

Dave squinted to focus below him and saw movement in the cloud but could not tell what he was seeing. "What is it general?" he asked.

"Ka-la-a," De-o-Nu gasped. That word did not translate. "Let's check it out, general. Let's go Charlie," and the Galliceans dived again. As they dived, Dave began to notice that the Galliceans were a bit smaller than before. The rising gas pressure was squeezing them already. Dave checked the pressure level in his heads-up display which reported normal. They passed through a grayish layer of clouds and saw a vast plain, seemingly floating in the sky. Rumbling along on the surface were massive creatures that looked like jellyfish, except without the long tentacles. "Now this is why we're here, Brother!" the captain said breathlessly. "I've never seen Ka-la-a like this."

"De-o-Nu," Charlie said, "what exactly is Ka-la-a? Our translators didn't work on that word."

Chapter 12

The Galliceans landed on the surface and folded their wings. "Ka-la-a is an ancient Gallicean word for floating islands," the captain began. "Like this one, they are made from suspended methane and water ice crystals that accumulate over long periods of time. As Gallia became industrialized, the atmospheric temperatures rose and the Ka-la-a disappeared. Fortunately, we had already developed the technology to build different kinds of floating islands. If not, all the Galliceans would have likely starved to death."

The general continued, "The growth on the ice begins as microscopic creatures floating in the gas, taking nourishment from the gas and other organisms in the flotsam. Once they land here, they continue to evolve into the moss-like growth here." He grabbed a handful of the moss and chomped on it. "Delicious!" he said. "I haven't tasted anything this good in a long time." As they spoke, one of the jellyfish creatures moved slowly their way. It was the size of a large truck, and appeared to be eating the moss as well. "These animals developed from smaller species that float in the clouds eating whatever comes their way. When they land on a Ka-la-a, they find a bountiful food resource and start to grow. I have never seen one this big."

"Are they sentient?" Dave asked.

"No," he replied. "These creatures have no brain. They are just overgrown versions of their relatives floating in the gas. They can be dangerous though. If several of them surround you, you might be crushed by their weight. And I would not recommend taking a nap on the Ka-la-a, or they might eat you too!" the general laughed. "De-o-Nu, give the crew our coordinates and have them send some men to harvest a nice fresh dinner for everyone." The two Galliceans and their charges took to the air again. "Dave and Charlie, how are you doing? What are your air readings?" Both reported they were at sixty percent. "Great, there is one more place I want to see today, if you are up for it?"

"What place is that, Fa-a-Di?" Dave asked.

"The Red Spot, of course," he replied. There was no reply. "Silence means consent! Let's go De-o-Nu." Off they flew again as fast as their wings could carry them.

"I wanted to see that too, Brother," the captain stated as they flew at top speed. "Dave and Charlie, we call that type of thing a Dar-Fa. They are great storms that drive electricity through the whole planet. They are full of tornadoes that pull rich resources from deep in the atmosphere, often from the surface itself."

"The main Dar-Fa on Gallia is the reason we were able to develop as a society," Fa-a-Di jumped in. "When the people of Gallia first began to develop, they created towns on the Ka-la-a. The Ka-la-a sat on layers of gas more dense than the ice, which is why they floated. But our culture could not continue to develop as larger colonies would cause the island to sink. There were thousands of small colonies all over Gallia. One of our ancient kings, Fa-o-Kan devised a way to build our own islands using the skeletons of our relatives when they passed. Our skeletons were much lighter and stronger than the ice. Those islands could be much larger and support more people without sinking so low we are could not survive. Over the millennia, those colonies joined together to become nations. As moss and other flotsam landed on the islands, it built up and covered the bones, making a kind of top soil. It was not like we were living in a graveyard." Dave could now see a huge wall of red clouds looming in the distance. It stretched far beyond the horizon in both directions. Even this far away, he could feel Fa-a-Di's body being buffeted from side to side. They had risen quite a bit above the level of the Ka-la-a, and the two Gallicean bodies had swollen to their size on the platform.

Chapter 12

"Yes, it was the general's ancestor who gave us nations," De-o-Nu acknowledged. "But it was my ancestor, De-no-Ko, who discovered that some of the materials floating up in the Dar-Fa could be used to make even larger islands. He found a way to convert what we now know to be solid lithium and other metals into platforms. They were many times lighter than even our skeletons. Once we began to build metal islands, our society developed rapidly until today." The captain was smiling broadly. "Brother, I recommend that we go as high as possible before we enter the Dar-Fa."

"I concur, lead the way Brother," he replied. The two soared upward. Dave looked below and saw the cloud layers slipping farther away. The sky above was getting darker as they approached the top of the atmosphere. He glanced over at Charlie, who smiled back at him.

"Great ride, huh Dave," Charlie smiled. Before he could answer, both Galliceans dived into the Red Spot. They were buffeted about wildly and both men held onto their harnesses for dear life. Swirling bands of red zoomed about their heads and the howling of the winds was deafening even through their helmets. The Galliceans were very quiet, even though they seemed to be enjoying the ride. Suddenly, all the wind stopped and it became very quiet. They appeared to have entered a huge area of calm winds. All they could see were the red swirling walls in every direction. Dave looked down and was amazed. All around them were the tops of countless tornadoes that disappeared deep into the redness below. The captain and general signaled to each other, selecting the best funnel, and dove again, directly into the open mouth of a tornado.

Again Dave and Fa-a-Di were being viciously pushed about by the swirling winds. Dave could feel the wash of material flying up through the funnel toward the top of the tornado. He saw the general's body shrinking as the mounting atmospheric pressure pushed in on him. "Dave, clench your left fist if you get too much pressure," the general told him in a calm voice.

"You must love this, general," he replied. "I've never seen anything more amazing than this."

"Just wait a minute, Dave, the highlight of the trip is coming up real soon," the general said. After what seemed like a second, the general folded his wings against his body and plunged through the wall of the tornado. The thunderous sound of wind blocked Dave's mind. He could think of nothing else. He closed his eyes and thought of clenching his fist. Then the sound stopped. Dave opened his eyes.

They were out of the funnel, flying through a torrential down-pour. Liquid splashed all over both of them. Dave thought it must be methane, but did not know for certain. As far as the eye could see, there were hundreds or thousands of funnel clouds, reaching far above them and impossibly far below. Lightning crackled everywhere. There must have been thousands of strikes per second in this massive storm that stretched to every horizon. The flashes came from every direction and lit the bright red sky around them. There was the sound of thunder, but it was muted by the rain and wind. From time to time, Dave could see Charlie riding with De-o-Nu, backlit by lightning. They flew for some time, and the scene was constantly changing, but always the funnels, lightning and the red gas in all directions. Dave thought he could stay there forever. "Dave, I read your air supply at fifteen percent," Fa-a-Di said. "We'd better head back to the platform."

"Thank you General," Dave replied. "This has been the most amazing day in my life. You and De-o-nu have shown me a world that I never would have imagined. In my time, all of this would have been thought to be impossible. I am so grateful you are here and that you chose to share this adventure with me. It would be an honor if you would call me Brother."

"Thank you Brother Dave," he said as they flew off toward the platform.

CHAPTER 13

Dave sat quietly in his ready room on the Reliant. After returning from Jupiter, he had taken a long hot shower and put on a fresh uniform. Wearing that pressure suit for several hours had been hot and exhausting. He felt more relaxed now as he flipped through a stack of papers in front of him. It was Cadiz and Charlie's first report on the situation with the lost colonies. Dave was hardly reading the words. His mind was still full of the adventure on Jupiter. It had been a few months since he met Charlie and came to the future. He could not believe that his life had changed so much in so little time. The accountant from twenty-first century San Diego was about to embark on an interstellar colonization effort in the thirty-second, on board massive ships that would carry humanity to new corners of the universe. Two hours ago, he had been secured in a harness against the chest of a giant bird-man from a gas giant planet five thousand light-years away. Even as the thoughts raced through his mind, he was not certain whether they had really happened, or if he had simply lost his mind. A tone signaled that someone was waiting on the other side of the door. He pushed a button on the table and the door slid open.

"Dave," Charlie said as he entered with Cadiz, "Wasn't that the most amazing thing ever? It was so surreal that I felt like I was dreaming the entire time. And the Red Spot! Thousands of tornadoes and driving methane rain all around, battering us about. I know I was there, but it seems impossible." The two men sat across from Dave.

"You're right, Charlie," Dave began, "Ever since I've been back here, I keep wondering if it happened or if I have gone mad. I'm glad to hear at least one other person had the same experience.

That's a relief. Okay, guys, tell me about your report." As Dave finished, another tone sounded. He pushed the button again and Ensign Lamont Landrue entered with a large container.

"Admiral," Lamont said, "this offering was sent to you by General Fa-a-Di." He opened the container and withdrew a dinner plate with food on it. "He said this food was from your visit to Jupiter. He had his personal chef prepare it for you and Charlie. The general asked that we send it to our science team first to make sure it was edible by humans. We have found nothing harmful. The general asked me to offer his kind regards as he had to jump back to Gallia for other business."

The large plate contained what appeared to be steamed greens and a slab of meat. The meat was pale pink and translucent. Dave looked at Charlie and then at Lamont. "Lamont, did you try it?" he asked.

"No Dave, I did not, although I did oversee all the testing in the lab. We were very thorough. While we could test for pathogens, we could not really assess flavor," he said. "I hope you enjoy it." Lamont left the room.

"Cadiz, I know the general said this was for Charlie and me, but please, go ahead and try it," Dave said.

"After you, Admiral," he replied, pushing the plate toward Dave.

Dave stared at the plate from some time, and finally picked up one of the forks that were in the container. He pushed around some of the greens, trying to figure out how they might taste. The scent was pleasant. Finally, he picked up a forkful and shoved it in his mouth. "That's damn good," he said at last. "It's a little bitter, which I like, but very crunchy, savory and spicy. It tastes a bit like kale and arugula at the same time." Encouraged by his reaction, Cadiz and Charlie each picked up a fork and tried the greens. Dave considered the slab of meat. In his mind, he saw the truck size jellyfish beast on the Ka-la-a. He was able to cut a piece of the meat using his fork. At least it was going to be tender. It smelled something like roasted pork. He put it in his mouth. "You know, that's not bad either," he said. "The flavor is a lot like pork. The texture is a little gelatinous though. This would take some getting used to." The others tried the meat as well, now that Dave had been the guinea pig.

After their tasting, Cadiz and Charlie updated Dave on the piracy situation at Day's End. Cadiz told him that Defiant and Courage had jumped to Day's End three days earlier and their captains had been meeting with the planetary council about the situation. There was usually an incident once every four or five days. Local defenses could not match the capabilities of the captured Kalidean ship. There had been no casualties on either side during the confrontations, but significant amounts of goods were stolen. Most of the residents of Day's End were sympathetic to the Skyers. Many had left that planet themselves during the great exodus, and still had family and friends on the renegade colony. When Captain Crain Crenshaw of the Defiant told the council about Dave's plan to rebuild Far Sky and New Dawn, they were very happy and relieved.

"What do we do now, Cadiz?" Dave asked.

"I think we need to meet with the leaders of Far Sky, and find out how we can proceed," he replied.

"How exactly can we do that?" Charlie jumped in.

"I have a plan that will probably require the help of your new brothers," Cadiz said. "Even our newest ships will have problems with a Kalidean cruiser. Their technology is far above ours. But if we had the help of several Gallicean starships, we would have the upper hand. Once we have that ship, the Skyers will have a real reason to listen to us."

"I like the way you think, Cadiz," Dave replied, smiling widely. "Let's set it up."

CHAPTER 14

Jon Lake was a pirate and the master of the starship Nightsky. The Nightsky, formerly known as the Kalidean cruiser Manila had been modified to accommodate its new crew. Several decks had to be removed as humans had difficulty with the low ceilings. The cargo bay had been greatly expanded to hold more supplies taken from the unsuspecting people of Day's End. Jon had not always been a pirate. His mother had been pregnant with him when his family had migrated from Earth to the new colony. He had attended universities on Day's End, and held a medical degree and Ph.D.s in starship and biomedical engineering. He had returned to Far Sky after college to help grow the colony by building hospitals and clinics. Twenty short years after his return, the supply ships stopped coming and the exodus began. His city, New Dallas, declined from one hundred thousand to ten thousand during the exodus. His family moved to the countryside and began farming to provide food for the region. Waves of disease moved across the land as medical supplies dried up.

Five years ago, a group of local residents came to him for help. A Kalidean ship had been captured in New Dallas. The locals knew Jon was highly educated and asked for his help in getting the ship ready. Jon did not like the thought of piracy, but he also saw the effects of rampant disease on his neighbors and family. He had to do something, so he moved back to the city and took command of the operation to restore the ship. His knowledge of the Kalidean language and engineering were instrumental in rebuilding the ship in four years. The Skyers suffered more with each passing day, but the project could not be rushed. Too much was at stake to allow haste to destroy their chance to get more food and medicine for the suffering people of Far Sky. He could see the faces of the Skyers each time they unloaded the supplies they had taken from

Day's End. Jon did not feel like a pirate. The people of Day's End did not resist their intrusions. They knew the situation on Far Sky was desperate. Many of them had lived on Far Sky themselves, but chose to leave in the great exodus.

"Jon, Day's End is visible on the view-screen," said Ali Bai, his first mate from the control console. "I'm also reading two star cruisers in the vicinity. Earth must be worried about us."

"Ali, steady as she goes," Jon responded. "Those cruisers can't match this ship and they know it. Try to find a target on the other side of the planet though. No sense taking any chances." Ali adjusted the course and moved the ship around to the far side of the planet.

"They have seen us for sure by now, Jon," Ali said.

"Don't worry, Ali," he replied. "Just keep an eye on them. If they start to come after us, we'll just zip out of here."

"Aye, aye, Captain," Ali said. "Steady as she goes." The cruisers did not move as the Nightsky slipped around to the night side of Day's End. "There is a depot at New Salem that looks promising. The data shows they were just restocked two days ago. It should be a piece of cake. I'm taking her in now." The Nightsky slipped into the atmosphere and dropped quickly into the thick cloud cover.

"Frake, we're landing in five minutes at the depot," Jon said into his communicator. "There are two star cruisers on the other side of the planet, so you have to make this very fast. Are you ready to go?"

"Always ready, boss. You know me," boomed the voice over the communicator. Frake Landres led the landing parties. He was a seven foot burly man whose mere presence made the locals forget about resisting. He had trained his crew of twenty to move quickly and quietly, always trying to avoid confrontations. Prior to his life of piracy, Frake had been a farmer, a poet, and a highly skilled cellist. Desperation had separated him from his instrument, which was now replaced with a laser rifle strapped across his back.

As the ship touched down, the twenty pirates hit the ground running. Frake was at the front, and ran to the security post, stopping cold. At the gate, in charge of security was his younger brother, Vance, who had moved back to Day's End during the exodus. The two men hugged each other. Vance pushed the button that opened the supply building. "Say hi to Mom when you see her," Frake said as he led his men inside. Within five minutes, the hold of the Nightsky was full and the crew was inside.

Ali launched the ship back into the sky. Within a minute she was back in space. "Jon, the two cruisers are starting to follow us," Ali warned.

"Bring up the speed to seventy percent," Jon advised. "There's no way they can go that fast. Say goodbye to Day's End men."

The ship accelerated and the two cruisers started losing ground to the Nightsky. They were barely visible in the rear view-screen when dozens of alarms started blaring on the bridge. "What the heck is going on now, Ali," Jon shouted over the din.

"Captain," he replied, "we have twenty Gallicean starships surrounding us. I have no idea where they came from. We're trapped."

A loud squeal poured over the speakers. Ali switched on the translator. "Hello, my friends," boomed the voice. "I am Captain De-o-Nu of the Gallicean starship, Kong-Fa. There is no escape from my fleet. I demand that you surrender your ship to me." The view-screen image of the fleet was replaced by the hawk-like face of the Gallicean. "Please do not make me waste any more time."

Jon looked at Ali. "What can we do?" he whispered. "We can't fight twenty battleships?" Ali shrugged his shoulders.

"You've taken too long," De-o-Nu said. At that moment, five Galliceans wearing battle ready pressure suits jumped onto the bridge of Nightsky, weapons at the ready. "Fifty more of my soldiers are all over your ship by now. Please surrender."

"I surrender the Nightsky to you, Captain," Jon said at last.

"Wonderful my friend," De-o-Nu shouted, laughing heartily. "We will stay with you until the Defiant and Courage can reach us. Then we will turn you over to them. Kong-Fa out."

CHAPTER 15

Jon Lake sat in Captain Lauren London's ready room on the Courage. He and his crew had been taken to the Courage when it arrived at the scene of the Gallicean ambush two days earlier. He had been kept in a separate cell in the ship's brig from his crew. That gnawed at him. He desperately wanted to know what had happened to them and his ship. He was angry at himself because he had not turned about when Ali first told him about the two cruisers orbiting Day's End. Perhaps he could have avoided the confrontation if he had not been so sure of himself and the Nightsky. The people of Day's End must have very strong connections in the galaxy in order to get twenty Gallicean starships to mount the attack.

The door slid open and Captain Lauren entered with two other humans. Jon knew they must be human, but they looked so different. They were quite short and very pale-skinned. Perhaps they were part Kalidean. The captain was showing great deference to the two, so he thought they must be very important. Jon had met Lauren when he was taken on board the Courage. She was a stunningly beautiful woman, very tall and shapely, with large eyes the color of coal.

"Admiral," she said to Dave Brewster, "this is Jon Lake, the captain of the pirate ship."

Dave walked around the table and put his hand out to Jon, saying, "How do you do, Jon? My name is Dave, and this is my friend Charlie." Jon nodded his head and limply shook Dave's hand. "We need to talk to you about the Far Sky and New Dawn colonies."

"First, tell me about my crew and my ship, Admiral," Jon replied. "The Skyers needed those supplies. People will be dying there soon if we don't get the shipment to them."

Dave and Charlie sat at the table across from the pirate. Lauren sat with them. "Your ship?" she shouted at him, "You stole that ship from the Kalideans who had come to help you. And now you call it your ship?" Both Lauren and Jon were turning red with anger.

"Calm down everyone," Dave said in a muted tone. "There is no need for that now. We have a great mission ahead of us, and we need to focus on that. Jon, I know you were doing what you needed to do to help the colonists that Earth deserted. The exodus was a shameful time for everyone. Your people suffered needlessly, and we are here today to fix that."

"My crew and ship, Admiral, answer the question," Jon replied.

"We brought a crew of Kalideans with us on the Reliant," Charlie began. "The ship has been turned over to them. They wanted you to know that they found the modifications you made to be of excellent quality. They plan to keep the larger cargo bay, although they thought the ten foot ceilings were a waste of valuable space."

Dave chimed in, "Your crew and the medical supplies have been returned to Far Sky, along with a few thousand more tons of supplies we brought from Earth. Without a ship, and knowing we are here to help your people, we doubt they will be much of a piracy threat in the near future."

"And I am to be tried as a criminal, no doubt," Jon said. "I don't care if you do. I did what I did because my people were in trouble."

"No one is trying anyone, Jon," Dave continued. "Lauren, please open the viewing port." She touched a button on the table, and the wall slid back showing a massive starship several hundred meters away. The ship was so large it filled half of the window. They could also see two other star cruisers nearby. All of them appeared to be orbiting above Far Sky colony. "Jon, that is my colony ship, the Ticonderoga. Two more ships like it will be ready to come here in a few weeks. The Council for Humanity has agreed to build at least seven more such ships."

"That's great for you, Admiral, but why are you telling me all of this," Jon asked. "If you're not going to prosecute me, please let me go to Far Sky now."

"You're not a patient man, are you Jon? I already told you we have brought along more supplies than you could have stolen in a hundred more raids. I would have thought you would be happy about that at least," Dave asked.

"Well, Admiral," he began, "if it is true, then I'm grateful. All I have is your word that you did that, and released my crew. Why should I believe you? And by the way, what planet are you guys from, Admiral? You're so short and pale. You don't look healthy at all to me. Perhaps the supplies you gave us did that to you."

Charlie and Dave laughed out loud. "It's not where we are from that did this," Charlie laughed. "It's when we are from. Dave and I were born in the twentieth century. We were asked to jump here to kick start humanity's expansion into the galaxy. Dave the Explorer here is going to found a thousand worlds!"

"Right now," Dave started, "I'm not interested in founding any new worlds until we fix the mess we inherited. Jon, I need your help to manage the re-colonization of Far Sky and New Dawn. I am going to commit my entire fleet to fix the mess that we stuck you and your friends with. I told High Commissioner Darak I plan to relocate at least a billion people to each planet."

"Holy crap!" was all that Jon could say.

"Jon, I couldn't agree with you more," Dave said. "Every day since I found out about these colonies, I've been feeling guilty about what happened. And it happened a thousand years after I was born! There was nothing I could have done in my time to fix this. Now, in your time, I will do whatever I can to get it right this time. Are you with me, Jon? And for goodness sake, please call me Dave."

Jon looked down and thought for a moment. Then he raised his head and stared into Dave's eyes, saying, "Dave, if all of that is true, I am with you."

"Fantastic!" Dave shouted. "Lauren, send Jon back to Far Sky on a shuttle right away. Jon, please think about this some more. On Far Sky, meet with your crew and you can confirm everything I've said so far. Charlie and I will visit you in a couple of days. If you are still ready to help us, we can start then."

They all rose from the table. Lauren signaled Jon to follow her. As he passed Dave, he said, "What if I decide not to help, Dave? What will happen to Far Sky?"

"Jon, my friend, either way I'm going to do the same thing. Within a year or two, there will be a billion more Skyers building factories and farms, and leading healthy lives as an active part of the community of man. You have done so much here to help these people. You have the knowledge and skills to do great things. When Chief Engineer Lagerfeld told me how I will be viewed in the future as Dave the Founder of a Thousand Worlds, I did not believe it. I'm an accountant from twenty-first century

Earth. If I had the same skills as you, I might have believed it. But I still came. I was given the opportunity to do great things for humanity. Now, I hope I am giving that same opportunity to you. This opportunity could lead to a wonderful vibrant Skyer community, or you may choose to follow Charlie and me and found those other thousand worlds. Or, you can return to your farm and be happy there. It's okay, as long as you are happy with your choice." Dave shook Jon's hand heartily. "Take care friend, and we'll see you down below in a couple of days."

Jon, Lauren and the two guards left Charlie and Dave alone in the ready room. The two men walked over to the viewing window and looked at the scene outside. "Charlie, you know," Dave began, "this still seems like a dream to me. Here we are, twenty light-years from Earth, orbiting another world that will soon be full of people because of what you and I are about to do."

"Aria always told me that life in this time would be hard for me to accept," he replied. "But that's not true. Life here is good. It's completely crazy and unbelievable, but still it's very good. The way you talked to the pirate was amazing. I think Jon will be happy to help us now. It's as though you offered to let him do everything he had ever wished he could do."

"I hope so Charlie," Dave said putting his hand on Charlie's shoulder. "We need leaders like him to help us bring the Skyers back into the fold. They also know what Far Sky is like, warts and all, and can help the new immigrants settle and fit in. Sometimes, I'd like to let this all go and just go home and keep looking for a job as an accountant."

"Do your really think you might do that, Dave?" Charlie asked.

"No, probably not. This existence is too amazing to give up. I still want to fly with Fa-a-Di again, only the next time it will be Saturn, or maybe Gallia," Dave replied.

"Well Dave, right now, I'd settle for a nice cappuccino, and maybe a chocolate croissant," Charlie said as they walked out the door.

CHAPTER 16

When Jon Lake landed on Far Sky, the shuttle craft was met by a large crowd at the star dock. He saw Ali, Frake and the rest of his crew waiting to welcome him back. His sister, Aliz, was at the front of the crowd and rushed to hug him when he stepped out of the shuttle craft. They told him the city was holding a banquet in his honor and they pulled him along toward the town square. Residents of New Dallas lined the streets and joined in the crowd as he passed by. Everyone wanted to shake Jon's hand and pat him on the back. At the town square, picnic tables had been set up and a banquet line of food and drink was awaiting them.

Jon was led to a table on a dais, and sat at the appointed spot. Aliz and Frake sat on either side of him. Soon the throng of five thousand had been seated. Everyone was smiling and talking to their neighbors about the events of the last few days. A group of waiters, townsfolk as well, moved through the gathering pouring local wine in everyone's glasses and passing out plates of appetizers. The waiters then sat to join the festivities. Alton Brae, the Mayor of New Dallas, rose and walked over to Jon and his crew and shook each hand, offering his sincere congratulations on their success. He then moved over to a podium that had been wired for sound.

"Good day, fellow Skyers!" he began. The crowd erupted in cheers and shouts. Alton waved his hand to get order, and continued, "Today, we are here to celebrate the glorious crew of the Nightsky, who have helped us to reach a turning point in the history of New Dallas and all of Far Sky." More cheers pierced the air. "Many of us had become resigned to the eventual end of this colony over the many years since the exodus decimated our numbers and the supply ships stopped arriving. I had come to accept that as well. We had no chance of survival without the needed medical and other supplies. Our society was doomed to turn back to earlier times with a terrible quality of health and life for those of us left behind. It was our choice, but it did not look like it had been a good choice." The mayor pointed to Jon and the other pirates at the head table. "Then one day, our great friend, Frake the Brave, led a group of fellow Skyers and took possession of the Kalidean ship, now renamed Nightsky." Shouts and applause rang around the square. "Frake, please stand up and take a well deserved bow." As he stood, the crowd erupted in applause and shouting that lasted five minutes. Frake blushed bright red and waved to the mass of people. The mayor continued, "We had the tool then, but no way to make it happen." He waved at Jon to rise as well. The shouts grew louder still. "And then this man came to our rescue. Jon the Commander and his team converted that research ship into a great pirate vessel." Applause filled the air. "Not only that! Then Jon Lake led this crew on a hundred missions to get the medical supplies that we needed so desperately. Jon, come on up here and say a few words!"

The thunderous applause and shouting lasted for minutes before Jon could hear anything else. He waved to the crowd and pointed to different people whom he knew or were part of the team that rebuilt the ship. When the noise dropped, he said, "Thank you Mr. Mayor. Thank all of you for your support of my crew. We only did what any right minded person would have done. It was an honor to help the people of Far Sky overcome the hardships put upon us. When I started this mission, I firmly believed some day war ships would come to stop us. But, I was certain that battle would destroy the Nightsky and my crew. I was prepared for that. I was not prepared for what did happen. Earlier today, I met with two people from the twenty-first century." Quiet murmurs filled the air. "They have said many wonderful things I hope are true. If so, today marks the new beginning of a great history of Far Sky colony. I will continue to do everything in my power to help that future come true for all of us. My sister, my crew and I thank you for this wonderful occasion and your dear company."

After another wild round of applause and shouting, the Mayor shook Jon's hand and joined him at the podium. He put his arm around Jon's shoulder, saying, "Jon, I have here in my hand a document signed by both High Commissioner Darak Daniels and Admiral Dave Brewster. This document says that Far Sky will hold elections for a High Council within six months. Only residents who have lived on Far Sky for at least five years will be able to vote or hold office. Any new colonists will have to wait until the third such election to meet this condition. Therefore, we will control the destiny of our planet for at least the next eight and one-half years." The crowd cheered yet again. "The document also says that Darak and Dave have selected an Interim High Commissioner for Far Sky for the six months before the first election." The crowd grew very quiet. "And that person is Jon Lake!"

The celebration lasted long into the night. Messages were sent to all of the settlements on Far Sky about the events at New Dallas. Thousands of congratulatory messages were sent to Jon Lake. He was happy to find his family and friends safe and happy. The food was wonderful and the wine was even better. He knew much of the wine was from his own vineyard. While surrounded by Gallicean soldiers, he had thought he would never taste that again. So far, Jon had found that Dave was telling the truth. The future would tell.

CHAPTER 17

Six months had passed since Jon Lake was released and sent back to Far Sky. Dave Brewster had remained in orbit on the Ticonderoga, coordinating the arrival of colony and construction ships. He communicated with Jon and his teams daily, but stayed on board so that Jon could remain the leader of his planet. The reestablishment of Far Sky was going very well. Thousands of new structures had been completed, and many more were constantly under construction. More than one hundred thousand people had already migrated from the inner planets to Far Sky, doubling its population. Another hundred thousand were involved in the construction projects. Some would remain, but most were expected to return to their homes when their jobs were completed.

Dave felt all alone orbiting in space above Far Sky. He had sent his friend Charlie with the Reliant to New Dawn to assess that planet. Jon Lake had known very little about the other colony. No one on Far Sky had any contact with them. Aria and Darlene had jumped back to the twenty-first to start convincing their children to move to the future. They knew convincing them to leave Earth would not be simple. They had no idea their parents had moved to the future and seemed content to keep their lives just as they were. Dave knew their mothers could have more impact on them than Charlie or him. Aria was a question mark though. She was not the mother of Charlie's children. With his friends away, Dave was feeling lost and lonely on the ship with its crew of ten thousand. He longed to walk those few blocks from his twenty-first century home to Starbucks and chat with Charlie again. A tone sounded, indicating an incoming transmission. Dave touched the control button and the view screen came to life. He saw High Commissioner Jon Lake smiling at him. "Jon, how are you today?"

"Very good, Dave," he replied. "I just wanted to give you a quick update on the election preparations." Dave nodded, and Jon continued, "Everything is coming together well. All the polling locations have been set up and the voting equipment is on its way from Day's End. That stuff should arrive tomorrow or the following day at the latest."

"That is good news Jon. What is going on with the candidates?" Dave asked.

"It's about as good as we could have expected," he replied. "We have five hundred candidates for the regional councils for three hundred positions. After the election, the thirty regional councils will each select one councilor to be on the planetary High Council. That council will then select the High Commissioner. I've personally met most of the candidates, and I think we have a great field."

"Are you getting any negative feedback from newcomers to Far Sky? Are they upset that they can't vote?" Dave queried.

"Some, but that was to be expected," Jon said. "I think our communications about how well our candidates understand this planet from years of experience and are committed to making everyone a partner in our progress has minimized the issue."

"That's good, Jon," Dave said, calmed that the new Skyers were not frustrated by the rule. "I hear you are doing very well in the polling in the New Dallas region. I knew that would happen. You've been doing a great job there Jon. Darak and the entire High Council are thrilled you decided to help us."

Jon's face looked pained. He looked down, and then back at Dave. "Dave, thank you for the vote of confidence, but to tell the truth, I'm not sure I was cut out to be a High Commissioner, or anything else in government."

"Are you thinking about dropping out of the contest?" Dave asked, very surprised by this turn of events. "Of course, I do remember what I told you on the Courage when we first met. All we really want is for you to be happy, Jon. It's up to you to decide if that's in government or on your farm. It would be a big loss for the growth of Far Sky, in my opinion."

"Or maybe my place is in space, Dave?" Jon said. "I've been talking to Aliz and Frake a lot about this. I am so grateful to you for what you are doing for Far Sky that I can never say thank you enough." Dave smiled and nodded his head. Before he could speak, Jon began again, "But I've been thinking that I could do a lot more for humanity by helping you found those thousand planets. I've never been much for meetings and setting rules and regulations. I'm more of a builder and problem fixer. When I was retrofitting the Manila, I recognized how much I love space and the adventure to find new planets and new civilizations."

"It does seem like a pretty glamorous idea," Dave said. "But the truth is that it is a lot of work and negotiations and time spent away from home."

"Admiral, do you want me to help you and Charlie or not?" Jon said flatly, smiling.

"Jon, I would be honored if you would join us on this adventure. Welcome to the team, Captain Jon," he said with a beaming smile crossing his face as well. A second tone sounded on the control panel. Dave recognized this as a high priority message coming in. "Jon, I've got to take this call. I'll shuttle down there this afternoon. Perhaps I can have dinner with you and Aliz later?"

"Aye-aye, Admiral, we'll see you then," Jon replied, "Far Sky out."

Jon's image disappeared, and after a second was replaced by the smiling beak of De-o-Nu, the new governor of the Gallicean planets in the Earth's solar system. "Brother Dave, how wonderful to see you again, my friend," he said.

"Brother De-o-Nu," Dave replied. "It is great to see you too. I trust you are well and happy on Jupiter?"

"I was just flying through the Red Spot again this morning," he laughed, "I remembered our first journey there with you and Charlie Watson. What was wonderful place! My people are amazed at the amount of resources we have found on this planet. It was a true blessing that we have been given this opportunity. But Dave, I have rather urgent news to report."

Dave looked concerned. "Is everything okay, Brother? Did something happen?"

"Everything is fine, Dave. But we have made a rather extraordinary discovery on the outer planets of Uranus and Neptune. As my brother, General Fa-a-Di may have told you, those planets are much too cold for us to inhabit," De-o-Nu started.

"Yes, I had heard that report as well, Governor," Dave said.

"Our scientists thought we could at least mine those planets for resources that might be useful for your people and ours. I dispatched the Kong-Fa with a small crew and a large group of scientists to check it out. They first examined Uranus, where they found very large extractable quantities of many excellent materials. However, the crew experienced serious feelings of anxiety and sorrow while there. Our doctors on the ship could not determine what was wrong. Immediately after they left, those feelings subsided. As they approached Neptune, the feelings returned and were much more severe," De-o-Nu said.

"That sounds very serious indeed, Brother," Dave replied. "Please continue."

"When they settled into a low orbit, those feelings disappeared, and were replaced by a constant buzzing in their heads, and we discovered what had really happened, Dave," the Gallicean said. "We were encountering telepathic messages from highly intelligent, sentient Beings on both planets."

Dave stood up at the table, stunned. "What! I can't believe it! Our people never detected anything and we've studied those planets for a very long time."

"I know Brother," De-o-Nu continued. "Our chief physician on Jupiter, the esteemed Doctor No-o-Ka believes that our biology is much closer to those Beings than yours. Both Galliceans and Neptunians are gas planet creatures. Our minds must have enough similarity to theirs that we can sense their thoughts. We don't know what they are thinking, but those telepathic transmissions appear as anxiety and sorrow in our brains. This is really amazing stuff, Brother."

"I am as astounded as you, Brother," Dave began. "What do we do now?"

"First, we have stopped all activity in the vicinity of those planets," the Gallicean started again. "We are assembling a team of scientists from Earth, Gallia and Kalidus on Io to work on the problem. Somehow, we must be able to translate those messages so that we can understand them. I have discussed this with General Fa-a-Di earlier today. We are also suspending any further colonization of Jupiter and Saturn until we can determine if there are Neptunians on those planets as well. We cannot harm or displace another sentient species."

"I understand and agree fully, Brother," Dave said. "This is indeed an amazing revelation. It is shocking to think that humans have lived so close to such a species for thousands of years and had no idea. Please ask the team of scientists working on this to keep me updated on their progress. I am so sorry, Brother. I sincerely hope this will not affect relationships among our people."

De-o-Nu laughed heartily. "Dave, there is no chance of that," he began. "What has happened here is the best possible news. The people of Gallia do indeed want to expand and grow our society. But one of the greatest aspects of expansion is finding new life and forming new relationships with Beings we never knew existed. These Neptunians are like brothers to the Galliceans. In all of our journeys, we have never found any new species of sentient life on gas planets. Many Galliceans were beginning to feel that we were alone in the universe, like freaks of nature. Now we have found new life that lives like we do. This is a great honor and joy for all Galliceans. We owe that to you and your wife, Ambassador Darlene. Thank you, Brother Dave." De-o-Nu smiled broadly. "Jupiter out." The screen went blank.

Dave sat quietly for a moment, trying to assimilate the information on Neptune and Uranus. This was a monumental discovery that could change the course of history for all life in the galaxy. He pressed a button on the control panel, and the smiling face of his communications officer, Lia popped up on his screen. "Yes, Admiral," she said, "What can I do for you?"

"Lia," he began, still impressed by the blue of her eyes, "can you find out when Aria and Darlene are due to jump back?"

"That would be tomorrow at 0800, Dave," she replied, "I've seen the schedules already."

"Great, then there is time for me to get there before then," he said. "Please send Chief Engineer Lanz a temporal jump request for two people. We need to go as quickly as possible."

CHAPTER 18

Bill Brewster was pretty certain his mother had gone crazy. When Darlene and her very tall friend Aria had arrived three days ago, he had been very happy to see her again. Since he had moved to Northern California four years ago to take his first job after getting his master's degree in biomedical engineering, he had only seen his parents on holidays. The first two days were totally normal. The two ladies had gone shopping in San Francisco, picking up items for his condo as well as some clothing for themselves. He had breakfast and dinner with them each day. He had been surprised how good a cook Aria was, but was very happy for the gourmet meals, compared to the microwave entrees he usually ate after a long, grueling day in the lab.

Perhaps it was the amount of wine they had all drunk with last night's dinner. His mother had started talking to him about traveling in time and Beings from the future and other planets. She was a lab technician from San Diego, who was married to an accountant. Now, he was supposed to believe they were living eleven centuries in the future. As a highly educated engineer, he knew that was not even possible. Yes, she must be mad. But what about Aria? Was she living in the same delusion his mother was? He rolled over in bed and tried not to think about it. The smell of brewing coffee and frying bacon drifted into his head. It was impossible to resist those scents. As he pulled on his jeans and a tee shirt, he realized the entire episode last night must have been a dream.

He walked into his kitchen to find Aria standing in front of the cooktop, managing several pans at once. He pulled a cup out of the cabinet and poured the fresh coffee. This was exactly what he needed to pull the cobwebs out of his mind. "Good morning, Aria," he said.

She turned around smiling and nodded. "What was she wearing?" Bill thought. It had seemed like a simple matching pair of slacks and top from behind, but when she turned, he had seen that it was more like a uniform. It had some form of rank insignia on the shoulders, and a number of other things pinned to the front. She wore a wide belt that had a number of strange devices clipped to it.

"Good morning Sweetheart," Darlene said as she entered the kitchen behind Bill. He turned to see his mother wearing a similar uniform, except there were only two small disks on the lapels, and she wore a red sash with odd symbols on it. She took a cup and filled it with coffee. She moved to the refrigerator to get the half and half and sat at the table.

"Ladies," Bill started, somewhat bewildered, "It's a little early for Halloween, isn't it?" Aria giggled as she opened the oven and pulled out a quiche. The fragrance filled the room. "Wow, Aria, or is it General Aria, that looks wonderful."

"It's Colonel, if you really want to know," she said as she cut a wide slice of quiche, added three strips of bacon and hash browns to the plate and slid it in front of him. "I didn't think the uniform thing was a good idea, but your mother insisted. I thought it would just be more confusing." She prepared two more plates for Darlene and herself, and joined them at the table.

"I am confused Colonel, you got that right," Bill started, "but I'm more worried that the two of you are medically confused, if you know what I mean." He took Darlene's hand and squeezed it. "Mom, you know I love you, but this is all pretty crazy. You know that, don't you?"

"Billy, I know it is confusing to you. How could you ever imagine any of this being true? I realized that last night after dinner," Darlene replied. "I can't believe it myself sometimes, but I have been living in the future for the last eight months. I have done things and seen things I thought were impossible. But it is happening. It is true."

"First, I just talked to you on the phone last week. Second, let's say I decide that it's true," he said. "What am I supposed to do with this information? Do I keep it a secret that my parents are flying through space and time a thousand years in the future? That part is easy! Everyone would think I'm nuts if I told them about any of this."

"Billy honey, I want you to come with us," Darlene said. "Your future is there and you and Cybil will do wondrous things."

"Pack my bags, sell the condo and fly into space, right?" he said, almost shouting. "What if I say no, Mom?"

"That's okay too, sweetheart," she replied. "Your dad and I only want you to be happy. Aria told that time is very resilient. If you don't do the things we know you can do, someone else will fill the void. Perhaps the results won't be exactly the same, but the future will move forward." Darlene motioned to Aria who pulled a small metal box from her belt and set it on the table.

"What the hell is that?" Bill said. "Is it a blaster or something to make me go?"

"Of course not, silly," his mother said, trying to calm him down. "That's a big reason Aria is here with me. I don't really know how to use all these things, and she is an expert in time and space jumping."

"Bill," Aria began, as she tapped buttons on the small device. "This machine can erase some of your memories of our visit. You'll remember almost everything, except the details of this discussion and the one last night. You'll remember how happy you were to have your mother visit, and what a great cook I am, but nothing about time travel and the rest."

"When will I see you again, Mom?" he replied with tears starting to fill his eyes. "Is this it now? Can I ever see you and Dad again?"

"Of course Bill," Darlene replied, stroking his hair. She stood up and wrapped her arms about him. "It's time travel, silly. We can come here for a couple weeks a year, with maybe a few short visits as well. But that's future time, son. To you, it will seem like we are just away a week or so at a time. For all you know, we might be on a cruise or something."

"But won't you and Dad get like fifty years older in one year of my time then? I think I might notice that!" he said.

"Bill, people live a lot longer in the future," Aria started, "I'm seventy five years old. My life expectancy is between four and five hundred years. Since Dave and Darlene have been living in the thirty-second, they've been treated with modern medications. There is no reason to believe that they won't live as long, or even longer if you end up in my time."

"That's the story from last night about Cybil and I fixing human DNA so people live to be a thousand, right?" he asked. Darlene and Aria nodded in agreement. "I don't know, Mom. This still seems like a big joke. I don't know if I'm prepared for that. Can I just say no for now, keep the knowledge and let you know in a couple days?"

Aria frowned in disapproval, but Darlene waved her off. "Sure Billy, if that's what you think you need. But you have to keep all of this very secret. If more people hear about this, we might have to erase memories from all of them. It could quickly get out of control. Okay?" Bill nodded his agreement, clearly relieved to have some time to think. "Aria and I have to visit her stepson Matt in San Diego for a couple of days. When we come back, you can give us your decision." Darlene smiled happily as she bit off a piece of bacon. "This really is excellent, Aria."

Bill's doorbell rang. As he left to answer it, Aria started, "Darlene, I think this is a bad idea. He's convinced we're crazy or something. It wouldn't surprise me if we came back and found ourselves in a mental hospital somewhere. I need to erase his memory before we go. It would be worth my rank to let him wander the area telling his friends and coworkers that his mother has gone insane." She continued tapping on the device on the table as Bill returned to the room, followed by Dave and Cybil.

Darlene rose and embraced her husband. "Dave, what are you two doing here?" she said. "This is an unexpected surprise." She hugged Cybil and kissed her cheek. "It's great to see you here baby."

"You see what I mean Dad?" Bill began, "Those outfits are pretty crazy, right? Have you ever met Aria before? She tells me she's a colonel. I think there's something very wrong here."

Dave considered the gathering in the small kitchen. "I have to agree with you son," he said. "Those outfits do seem out of place for Sunnyvale, California." He turned to Aria, saying, "Wouldn't you agree Colonel? I'm surprised you'd allow it."

"Dave, the ambassador was very demanding and convincing," she replied. "She thought this was the only way to convince Bill that what we are saying is true."

"Short of a jump of his own," Cybil responded. Bill was overwhelmed and sat heavily on a chair, holding his head in his hands. "It's okay, little brother," she continued, "I moved to the thirty-second three months ago."

"But I talked to you two days ago," Bill muttered.

"Time travel, silly," she replied. She sat next to her brother and rubbed his shoulders. "Maybe we are all really crazy. Maybe just you are. There's one way to find out. Come back with me and I'll show you so much in one day that you'll never want to come back."

"No time for temporal tourism now, kids," Dave interrupted. "Bill, I need your help right away. I want you to jump to the future with me now. I think you have unique skills that are desperately needed right now."

"You need my skills Dad?" Bill said. "Like what?"

"You were recently promoted due to your work on a project to allow amputees to control prosthetic parts using their brain waves, right?" Dave asked.

Bill nodded slowly, saying, "Yes, but the whole thing was dropped when the first trials were not that great and we couldn't get the funding we needed from Corporate."

"I seem to recall that a big part of the research focused on translating certain brain wave patterns into signals that could operate the devices," Dave continued. "You were trying to learn what individual mental signals meant, and then tie those to the mechanics of the prosthetic. The normal mental signal to move an arm would then move the prosthetic arm. That is what we need right now."

"Dad," Bill replied shaking his head slowly, "if you are really in the future, don't you already have better technology than that? I would be surprised if my twenty-first century education could add anything."

"As far as medicine is concerned, you're absolutely right, son," Dave acknowledged as he sat across from Bill and looked him in the eye. "If a person loses an arm, a new one can be grown from the stump of the old one within a few weeks. Son, what we need is your knowledge on decoding brain signals and finding ways to translate them. Believe it or not, the fate of three civilizations rests with our ability to do exactly that as soon as possible." Dave took Bill's hand and squeezed it tightly. Bill looked up and smiled as his father. "Son, I want you to go with me now. If I'm crazy, we'll just be walking out the door into the sunshine. Then you can take all of us to the asylum. If you end up in the future, you can work on this project and help us complete it quickly. When that is finished, you and Cybil can go on your vacation in the future, or if you prefer, you can come back here. I love you, Bill. I need your help. Please come with me now." Dave finished.

Bill Brewster looked around at his family and Aria all smiling at him warmly. He was almost convinced he was the crazy one now. "Sure, Dad, I'll go," he said at last. "I don't want to be the only sane person left. I might as well join the craziness."

"Thank you Billy," Dave replied. He turned to Darlene. "Sweetheart, I think you and Aria should continue your trip and catch up with Matt. Cybil, Bill and I are scheduled to jump to the Io Star Port on our signal."

"Okay, Dave," she replied. "Aria and I will take care of everything here. Billy, there are others from the thirty-second who can handle the loose ends if you're gone a while. Remember, it is time travel, so you could jump back in six months, and it would still be today here."

Bill answered, "If you say so Mom. I think it might take a long time for me to wrap my head around that! I'm still pretty sure that when I walk out the door, I'll still be here and it will still be now. But, how can a guy argue with both of his parents and his crazy sister? Doesn't this get confusing with people flying through time everywhere all the time?"

"Not really Bill," Aria replied. "There are very few people authorized to jump in time; less than fifty. This symbol on my shirt, with the wings and dial in the center shows that I am part of the Temporal Command. Only our members, and a few distinguished guests like the Admiral and Ambassador here get the chance. What they are doing for the people of my time is so miraculous that we have given them a lot of leeway." She turned to Dave, continuing, "I'm quite surprised that Lanz gave you the approval for this. It seems very unusual."

"Unusual doesn't begin to describe the situation," Dave answered. "The Galliceans discovered a new sentient life species on Neptune and Uranus." Aria, Cybil and Darlene looked shocked. Bill was so overwhelmed with thoughts that he let it pass over him. "That's why we need Bill now. The Galliceans can feel the thoughts of these Beings in their heads, but it's just gibberish. We've got to figure out what they are thinking quickly before we damage their civilization any more than we have already. Let's go kids." Dave rose and kissed Darlene, holding her in his arms. "Sweetheart, I heard you are jumping back tomorrow my time. I'll see you then. I love you." He turned to Aria and kissed her cheek. "Aria, thank you for your work, and I wish you all the success with Matt. Charlie tells me he is a tough nut to crack."

"Aye-aye, Admiral," she replied. Have a safe jump and I'll see you and Charlie tomorrow."

"Charlie's still on the mission to New Dawn. I'm hoping he'll return soon. I'll be on Io for a day and then jump back to the Ticonderoga," Dave said as he and his children walked out of the kitchen.

As they stepped into the living room, Bill said, "Well, should I pack something before we step out front?"

"That's okay, son," Dave replied, "We've got everything you may need in the thirty-second."

Bill noticed a small black dot on his front door. As he watched, it quickly grew to a seven foot circle. It was blacker than night and seemed as smooth as glass. "What the heck is that?" he blurted.

"Don't sweat it, bro," Cybil said calmly. "As you said, we're just stepping out the front door into the sunshine. Dad, I'll go through with Bill. You jump first." Dave smiled at them and stepped into the portal. "It's okay Billy," she said holding his hand. "We just step in, and then we step out. You won't be able to hear me when we are inside, but that will only be a second. When the opening on the other side is stable, we'll step through and be there." Bill looked anything but confident, but with his sister's hand in his and his father already gone, he smiled wryly, shrugged his shoulders and they stepped in.

CHAPTER 19

Dave Brewster was very impressed by the team already assembled on Io to work on the Neptune situation. The leadership of the task force included Chief Engineer Lanz Lagerfeld, the noted Kalidean scientist Machinus, and Gallicean physician No-o-Ka. For this project, the team reported to Governor De-o-Nu. They were all very happy to welcome Bill Brewster to the team and agreed to update Dave regularly. Major renovations had taken place at the space port since his flyover with Fa-a-Di six months ago. A large laboratory had been constructed with accommodations for the Galliceans. All the major rooms were double-sized, with large glass walls through the middle so the different species could work together without pressure suits. Residence halls had also been constructed to cater to their different needs for breathable air and food supplies.

While Cybil had taken Bill to settle in, Dave was summoned to a private meeting with the Governor. He was led to a private conference room that had a glass wall through the middle. As he entered, he could see De-o-Nu on the other side, sitting quietly, sipping on a drink. As he approached the conference table that was also split to be on both sides of the glass, he said, "Good day, Brother, it is good to see you again."

De-o-Nu rose and pressed his hand against the glass. That was the best handshake they could make through the wall. "Brother," he began, "thank you for meeting with me today. Please sit down. Would you like something to drink?"

"No thank you, Brother," Dave replied as he pressed his hand to the glass across from the other. "I think this is the first time I've seen a Gallicean without either a foggy lens or pressure suit on one of us."

"I have felt the same way about humans and Kalideans since the facility was finished," he answered. "This was a great accomplishment for all of us. I am convinced that this kind of close working relationship will do much for our mutual growth. I also want to thank you for bringing your son to join the team. He will be a great addition."

"You are welcome for that Brother," Dave said. "When I thought about the Neptune situation and what was needed, somehow he just popped into my mind."

"Yes, I agree," the Gallicean continued, "but there are some problems on Gallia related to the Neptune situation, Dave. There are elements on Gallia that believe that these Beings may be hostile. Several crew members have been interviewed by the press talking about the feelings of sorrow and anxiety that they felt around those planets. Some of our people think those were deliberately placed in our minds to test us. If these Neptunians can control our thoughts, they can attack us and keep us from defending ourselves."

"Brother, those Beings have existed in peace with humanity for all time," Dave argued. "Why would they pick a fight with an advanced society like yours when they could have dominated Earth easily, even before humans evolved?"

"Brother, I am not in agreement with those who believe there is danger here, please be assured of that." De-o-Nu rose and began to pace around his half of the room. "But our people are very political. It has not been that long since humans or Galliceans were power mad and warlike. If they sense danger, they may demand action. We could then lose our one chance to befriend another gas planet species."

"What does our brother, Fa-a-Di think of this situation?" Dave asked.

"The general agrees with us, Dave," he began, "but he is susceptible to political pressure too. His term as High Commissioner will end soon, and he wishes to be reelected. Dave, you must assure me what I am about to say is between you and me. Not even your wife or children can know this."

"You have my word, Brother," Dave said. "Unless humanity is in danger, of course. I could not sit by and allow that to happen."

"Yes, I agree. The High Council has ordered the Chiefs of Staff to send ten war ships to Jupiter. My brother argued strenuously not to do such a provocative action near our friends on Earth. They threatened to censure and remove him if he refused." Dave sat very quietly, unsure what all of this meant for humanity. "Those ships are now on their way. They were told not to jump into this region, as that would be readily visible to everyone here. They are traveling the old-fashioned way. It will take five weeks for them to arrive here. Those ships have orders to remain in a very high orbit around Neptune when they arrive. They are to take orders from only the Chiefs of Staff or the High Council. You have my word as your friend and my brother that I will never allow any action against humans. Before any decisions are made on the Neptunians, I will advise you and the High Council for Humanity." De-o-Nu sat heavily, his wings limp by his side. "Dave, there was nothing else any of us could do to stop this." He took another long drink from his glass and sighed.

Dave now rose and began pacing. "De-o-Nu, first I want to thank you for taking me into your confidence on this matter," he started.

"Second, it sounds like we have five weeks to decipher the Neptunian language. God willing, that will be enough time, my friend."

"God willing indeed, Brother," the governor said. He rose slowly and walked out of the conference room. Dave sat down, trying to figure out how to turn this situation around. Ten minutes later, his mind still blank, he rose and left the room as well.

In one corner of the ceiling on the Gallicean side, a crystalline spider-like creature moved after having witnessed the meeting. Its body was about six inches across with twelve long legs giving it an overall diameter of three feet. While the others had been in the room, it had been completely transparent. After they left, it started to emit a bluish glow. It unfolded gossamer-like wings and floated down to the table. It scurried over to De-o-Nu's glass. It extended a thin tendril into the liquid and tasted the heavy Gallicean whisky. The Being seemed to relish the flavor. The bluish glow increased to a blindingly bright white. The light vanished, and the spider was gone.

CHAPTER 20

After the jump and busy day, Dave needed food and sleep. He met Bill and Cybil at a dining hall in the star port. That room was also split by a large glass wall. Many tables were placed against the glass so human and Kalidean scientists could have a meal with their Gallicean counterparts. Dave had enough of collaboration for one day and picked a small table against a wall where he could focus on his children.

"Bill," he started, "how are you doing? This certainly isn't Sunnyvale anymore, is it?"

"No Dad, it isn't," Bill replied, "although I haven't yet ruled out the insanity thing. This is just wild enough to be a delusion. It's amazing that we're sharing the same one though." They all laughed.

Through the glass, they could see a number of Gallicean engineers and scientists sitting at their much larger tables and chairs. The average Gallicean seemed to be about fifteen feet tall, like the general. Their skin color was slightly bluish and iridescent. They kept their wings tightly folded against their backs. Away from the center wall, they could not hear anything from the other side. The Galliceans seemed to be enjoying their dinner as well. The Brewsters could see them laughing and patting each other on the shoulders. Neither they nor any of the others in the dining hall noted the crystal clear spider-like creatures that sat frozen on the ceiling. There were only four in the immense room, and no one was focusing on finding anything other than what was on their plates.

113

"Dad," Cybil began, "I'll stay here with Bill tomorrow, but I have to get back to my studies on Earth tomorrow night. Is that okay?"

"Sure, Honey," Dave replied. "It means the world to me that you helped me convince your brother to help out." Turning to his son, he continued, "Bill, it will take a couple days to get used to the routine here, but I'm sure you can handle it. Chief Engineer Lanz is a good friend. He is the one who came looking for your mom and me. If you have any issues, you can confide in him. Also, all of us are available pretty much 24/7 if you need to contact us."

"Thanks Dad," Bill said. "Cyb has taught me so much already. I think I can use the communicators pretty effectively. I really like the folks on the team I was assigned to. In fact, after dinner, I'm meeting up with them in one of the clubs that's been opened here. From Sunnyvale to Io in an afternoon is quite a journey."

"Not to mention fast forwarding eleven centuries, little bro," Cybil cut in. "Call me first if you need anything. I'm not as important as Mom or Dad, so I can jump over here pretty much any time." She smiled at her brother and continued eating.

"Dad, the food here is pretty good, but not nearly like what Aria made, she's pretty amazing," Bill noted.

"Yes, she is a special lady," Dave replied. "Your mom and I had dinner at her house before we came here. It was fabulous. I don't know where she finds the time to do that and her day job."

Cybil looked up and said, "Dad, duh, it's time travel." They all laughed.

After dinner, Dave hugged his children and then excused himself. He was now exhausted. He dragged himself to his room, changed to his pajamas and went to the bathroom to freshen up for bed.

Sensing he was out of the room, two crystalline spiders moved about the room, finding dark corners to sit and wait. They glowed blue and then fell totally transparent. Dave returned from the bathroom and climbed into the bed. He was so tired he would not have seen the spiders if they were bright red with flashing lights. Almost instantly, he was sound asleep.

The two creatures floated down from the ceiling and landed next to Dave on the bed. Each reached out a filament-like tendril that glowed blue and touched him.

Dave dreamed that he was flying again over a gas planet. This time it was not Jupiter. The whole planet was blue and he could feel the bite of cold gas on his exposed skin. Fa-a-Di was not there to carry him, but he was flying nonetheless. He could not imagine what kind of gas he was breathing, but it felt like ozone-rich air after a thunderstorm on Earth. He looked up to the sky and could see a very bright star. It looked like Venus does from Earth, but maybe twice the size. What a wondrous place this was! He felt totally at peace up in the sky over this alien world. The cold was biting, but he felt warm and content inside. He flew through banks of clouds and found ice particles forming on his body. They quickly blew off in the wind. He looked down, but could only see darker regions of clouds, not even a Ka-la-a to land on. He felt happy and at peace.

On the horizon he now saw thousands of blue lights floating in his direction. They became larger and larger as they approached, but he did not feel any fear. Soon they were all around him. They looked like glass balloons supported by lacy clear wings. They flew around him performing all kinds of acrobatic acts, as if trying to amuse him. He felt himself smiling and was warmed and comforted by their presence. The creatures led him around their world, and he followed gladly. They especially enjoyed flying through the bands of clouds. They seemed to absorb the ice crystals into their bodies for nourishment. He followed them on their acrobatic moves and had no problem keeping up.

After flying a while longer, the creatures changed and began to emit a violet light. Their motions became erratic as they whirled around him. He saw they were approaching a floating city in the distance. The city was in flames and rocked by explosions. From high above, he could see a massive star cruiser that was blasting the city from space. The creatures left him and flew toward the cruiser, as if trying to defend their city. Dave tried to follow them to help, but they were far ahead of him now. He could see the star cruiser change course and head for the creatures that were now bright red. A blast came from the star ship and hundreds of the creatures were blown apart. Now the cruiser was preparing a second blast, but this time aimed at him. He could not help himself. He had to attack the star ship after what it had done to the defenseless creatures. Hundreds more were flying with him and approaching the ship. Another blast shot from the ship and a bright white light sped toward him. He felt the piercing white-hot plasma hit him, burning through his skin.

Dave woke and sat up in a panic. He was drenched in sweat. He reached for a lamp and switched it on. Everything in his room seemed normal, but the dream was still pounding through his mind. He rubbed his eyes, and said, "Wow! It must have been something I ate." He rose from the bed and went into the bathroom. When he was gone, the two spiders appeared from under his bed. They glowed white, and disappeared.

CHAPTER 21

Fleet Admiral Arrin Adamsen had not slept well that night either. He had been informed by his intelligence staff that a group of Gallicean warships had left Gallia in the general direction of Earth. The ambassador to Gallia from the High Council for Humanity, Marku Magnuson had sent an inquiry to the Gallicean High Council, but the curt response mentioned only military exercises in open space. The admiral ordered a small ship to follow the fleet at a respectful distance and track their progress. As he sipped his morning coffee in his office in the Pentagon, he touched a button on his control panel. The image of Captain Cadiz Carlyle of the Reliant appeared before him.

"Admiral, sir, what an honor to accept your call," Cadiz said, clearly surprised to get a call from the head of the star fleet.

"Thanks, Captain," Arrin began. "Cadiz, I need your help."

"Of course, Admiral," he replied.

"I need the Reliant and Defiant to return to Earth as soon as possible," Arrin said. "Admiral Brewster can keep the Courage for now."

"Admiral, is there a problem that we should prepare for?" Cadiz questioned.

"Not that we know of, Cadiz. At least not yet," Arrin replied. "I'll have your orders sent this morning, and I'll copy Dave so he knows you are leaving. By the way, is there any news regarding the colony on New Dawn?"

"Commodore Watson and I are scheduled to meet with Dave later today," Cadiz said. "We just returned from New Dawn yesterday. The admiral was on Io then so we could not meet with him until today. He is due to jump here within the hour. I can tell you that there is little good news on New Dawn."

"Okay, Cadiz," Arrin cut in, "I'll wait to hear Dave's report later. I don't want to break the chain of command. When do you think Reliant and Defiant can be here?"

"If we leave in twelve hours, we should arrive in three or four days. Will that be adequate, Admiral?" Cadiz responded.

"That is fine, Captain. Please give my regards to Charlie and Dave. Earth out," Arrin finished as he touched the button to close the link and the screen went black. "Well, if the game is on, at least we have our pieces on the board now too," he said to himself. He took another sip of coffee and sat back, closing his eyes, trying to imagine a battle between the Galliceans and his starships. Arrin knew he was totally outgunned. The Galliceans had been in space for many thousands of years, and most of those years had been peaceful. From his days at War College, he knew the first expansion from Gallia had been a war of conquest. They had conquered several civilizations, even though they did not inhabit the gas planets the Galliceans wanted. When those civilizations resisted their dominance, war was the only solution. Arrin had advised High Commissioner Darak of the risk, who had in turn mentioned the problem to Mencius the Kalidean. Mencius told Darak that the Kalideans would stand by their human friends, although he discounted the possibility of any hostilities. Arrin was not so certain though. Ten warships coming to Earth without an invitation and avoiding the Io Star Port was a very provocative act. A tone sounded and he pushed the contact on his control panel.

"My dear friend Arrin, it is so good to see you again," said General Fa-a-Di, sitting before him with a wry smile crossing his beak. "How are you today?"

"General, it is good to see you as well," Arrin began, "but I have had better days than this, Friend."

"Whatever do you mean Arrin," he asked.

"Fa-a-Di, I think you know exactly what I mean," Arrin responded, looking for a reaction on the Gallicean's face.

Fa-a-Di rose from his seat and began pacing about his office. "Friend, officially I can only say that I do not know what you could mean." Fa-a-Di walked over to a cabinet and withdrew a glass and a decanter of Gallicean whisky and poured until the glass overflowed. He sat at the table and took a long drink. "Arrin, we have known each other for a hundred years or more, right?"

"That's right, Fa-a-Di. When we met, I was new out of the military academy. As I remember it now, our peoples held joint war games in Kalidean space. That was the one and only time I tasted Gallicean whisky. Pretty intense and nasty stuff, General."

Fa-a-Di laughed heartily, drained his glass and refilled it. "Arrin, I can tell you that Gallia has changed a great deal since the discovery of the Neptunians. For thousands of years, we have hoped and dreamed of finding another intelligent species on a gas planet. When we had almost given up, Dave and Darlene presented us with four planets. Now, only a week or so after discovering the Neptunians, all of Gallia has gone insane with fear."

"Fear, that's odd. I would have thought they would be happy to find them after looking for so long," Arrin replied. "It's the fulfillment of a very old dream."

"That's what I said, Friend," Fa-a-Di bellowed. "But believe me, here on Gallia, happiness is hard to find these days. I've been High Commissioner for ten years now, so I suppose it is my fault in some ways. Perhaps if we would have kept it a secret until we were better able to break the news to the common man, it might have been better."

"I doubt that, Friend," Arrin said. "Like on Earth, news travels very fast, and there is little the government or military can do to slow it down."

Fa-a-Di nodded, "True enough, Friend. But let me get to the reason I called. As you may know, my second term as High Commissioner is ending soon. I have decided to retire from both my military and governmental posts when it does."

Arrin looked shocked. He had greatly enjoyed his time working with the general. He had also been a very positive influence on the relationship between Gallia and Earth. "But General, you are still a young man. I think that Gallia needs your wisdom and leadership now more than ever."

"Thanks for the vote of confidence, Arrin, but as I said, things in Greater Gallia are not running as well as you might think," he began. "I don't believe the hysteria about the Neptunians was a random occurrence. There are elements in our society that want major change. We have learned so much from you humans and the Kalideans about a society based on freedom and learning, but that is a major change that not all Galliceans can accept. Many here crave the order and structure we used to impose on our people. Of course, what that really means is there are some

Galliceans who want power over others. The situation on Neptune is a minor issue that is now being twisted by some to instill fear and hatred in the populace. When people are angry and afraid, they look to leaders who promise to take care of the problems. But the cost is usually very high. I do not wish to be part of that."

"Friend, I don't know what to say," Arrin responded. "What will you do after your resignation?"

Fa-a-Di smiled again, saying, "I have recommended to the High Council and they have agreed that I be appointed permanent governor of Jupiter. It's a small, out of the way colony and the new leadership will be able to do what they want on Gallia and the other planets without my interference. They have also agreed to promote my brother-in-law De-o-Nu to Fleet Admiral of the Gallicean Star Fleet. It's good for him, and they can keep an eye on me through him."

Arrin nodded. "Well, friend," he said, "if you think that's good, I certainly wish you the best."

Fa-a-Di laughed again, draining his glass. "Thank you my dear friend," he started, "and I would love the opportunity to show you Jupiter like I did our mutual friend Dave Brewster." Arrin smiled. "Before I switch off Arrin, let me tell you one more thing," Fa-a-Di said in a near whisper, "I told the Council that if they take any military action against the humans that I will personally come after them with my own fleet. They know I have fifty ships or more that are fiercely loyal to me. Those crews would fly into the nearest star if I asked them to. You have my word on that, Friend. Gallia out." Fa-a-Di smiled again, and the screen went blank.

CHAPTER 22

For some reason, space jumps upset Dave Brewster much more than temporal jumps. After jumping on board the Ticonderoga, he felt miserable. He went to his ready room as quickly as possible and sat down heavily. The door slid open and Lia stepped in. She put a cup of cappuccino and a chocolate croissant in front of him. Dave considered the food, but thought he'd better wait until his stomach finished its jump. "Dave," she began, "Charlie and Cadiz are here to give you their report."

"Thanks, Lia, please send them in," he replied, still astounded by her blue eyes. He had forgotten he was going to ask Charlie about her "Hi, Dad" comment. He made a mental note not to forget again. Dave gingerly sipped the coffee, but pushed the pastry to the center of the table. When the two men entered, he stood feebly and shook their hands, grateful to sit again.

"Dave, those space jumps are still killing you, aren't they," Charlie said.

"Yes, and it's good to see you again too, Charlie," he replied. "Okay, Cadiz, I received the orders to move Defiant and Reliant back to Earth today. Are you and your crews getting ready?"

"Yes, Admiral," Cadiz replied. "We will be ready to leave within ten hours. By the way Dave, do you know why we are going there? It seems rather odd."

"Well, I have my own opinions," Dave responded, "but no facts. We'll just follow orders and see what happens. You two can go ahead with your report."

Cadiz was correct when he had told Arrin that the news was bad. After the exodus, New Dawn was left with a population of fifty thousand. The Reliant was able to find about forty population centers with a total population of fifteen thousand. Life expectancy had decayed to roughly eighty years, and living standards were terrible. Food shortages and disease outbreaks were commonplace events. Unlike Far Sky, the terraforming of New Dawn was never completed. As time went by, more and more land reverted to its natural barren state. Water supplies were drying up, and the people were forced to move frequently to find fresh water. The largest settlement was New Dublin near a vast fresh water lake of the same name. The lake was shrinking by five percent per year. The city of five thousand had been built on the shores of the lake, which was now twenty miles away from town. None of the original settlers were still living. Most survivors were third or fourth generation Dawners.

When landing parties first attempted to contact the settlers, they were attacked. A number of crew members were seriously injured. The settlers had created firearms from the materials on the planet. Any of the original weapons sent with them had fallen into disrepair. Cadiz had requested that the recently launched colony ship California bring supplies for the settlers. When it arrived, landing parties, heavily armed with stun rifles, took shuttles of food, water and medicines to the planet. That process was now ongoing, while the Reliant returned to Far Sky to bring the report and crew members who needed better hospital facilities. Thankfully, all the injured were expected to fully recover.

Dave sat through the presentation, and now had his head in his hands. "Wow," he said, "I thought that Far Sky was a nightmare. This is unbelievable to me. How do we fix this mess without getting anyone hurt or killed? I don't think a fleet of Gallicean cruisers will do the trick this time! I doubt those people even know Gallia or Earth even exists!"

Charlie looked about sheepishly, saying, "Well, Dave, I had one idea. Cadiz didn't agree with it though."

"Okay, Charlie," Dave replied. "Let's hear it."

"We sort of borrowed the Mayor of New Dublin," he said, with his eyes cast downward.

"And his wife," Cadiz chimed in. "She's the head of the police department."

"Huh," was all that Dave Brewster could say. He sat quietly, took a bit of the croissant, and said, "Okay, let's talk to them then." He touched the control panel, saying "Lia, please show our other guests in."

Drew and Corrine Baker were led in by two armed security guards. The Dawners wore shackles to keep them under control. The guards led them to the table and helped them sit down. It was obvious to Dave that the water shortage was acute on New Dawn, because the Bakers were filthy. Their aroma filled the room. They looked around the room, never having been on a space ship before. Dave noticed they both eyed his croissant. Dave touched the button on the panel, and said, "Lia, please get some food for our guests. Lots of pastries and water, please." She returned almost immediately and placed the food and drink on the table. She poured large glasses of water for Drew and Corrine and then left the room.

"Guards," Dave said, "please release their hands so they can drink." The guards frowned their disapproval but followed orders. Drew and Corrine looked curiously at the offering. Dave sensed their concern and poured himself a glass and grabbed a pastry. He drank and took a bite, chomping happily. Less afraid, they drank the water and stuffed their faces with the food.

Dave let them eat and drink for a while in peace. When they seemed more relaxed, he opened, "Drew and Corrine, I'm Dave Brewster. You are now on the Earth colony ship, Ticonderoga in orbit over the Far Sky colony. You have already met my friends, Charlie and Cadiz."

"You can measure a man by the quality of his friends, Dave Brewster," Drew said. "I don't know if I could call a kidnapper my friend."

"We have criminal penalties for what you and your henchmen have done, buddy," Corrine chimed in. "If we were on New Dawn, you'd all be in a lot of trouble."

"Believe me, folks, we are in a lot of trouble here too," Dave said. "We don't look kindly on kidnappers either." He frowned at Charlie. "For the moment, let's assume that it was done for the right reasons, and not jump to conclusions before we can have an adult conversation about why we are all here today." He turned to the guards, saying, "Please release their shackles and wait for us outside."

Cadiz said, "Admiral, I don't think that's a good idea."

"Let me worry about that, Captain," he replied. Your guards can watch the screen from Lia's office. If anything odd happens, they have my permission to stun everyone in this room, okay?" Cadiz nodded, and the guards complied and left the room.

"Thanks Admiral," Drew said, "can you please take us home now?"

Dave touched another button on his panel. "Aye-aye Admiral," said the voice of Jonas Jalecki, Captain of the Ticonderoga.

"Captain, please chart and lay in a course to New Dawn," Dave said. "One quarter speed please. I'd like to get our guests home by tomorrow."

"Aye-aye, course laid in," Jonas said. "We will need two hours to get all the crew on board and in position, Dave."

"Okay, make it so, Jonas. Brewster out," he finished, pushing the contact. He turned his attention to Cadiz. "Captain, I know you and the Reliant need to leave for Earth today, so you are excused. Please give my regards to Arrin when you see him." Cadiz left the room. Charlie sat next to Dave. "Drew and Corrine," Dave began, "As you heard, we will be leaving for New Dawn soon, and you have my personal guarantee you will be returned to New Dublin tomorrow morning. You should know that the Ticonderoga is a state-of-the-art colony ship with ten thousand crew members. If you try to escape or do anything else silly, it won't go well. Also, I think this will give Charlie and me the time to tell you why we are here, and why you are here with us, okay?"

"It seems we have no choice, Admiral," Drew said. He took another mouthful of pastry and chewed it ravenously. "It's not a bad place, and the food is good. Tell us what you want us to know."

Dave and Charlie told them everything, from meeting each other in a coffee house in the twenty-first century to the repopulation of Far Sky and the current situation on New Dawn. Dave told them about flying through the Jovian skies with Galliceans and the great works of Mencius the Kalidean in kick-starting humanity into the stars. He repeatedly apologized for the problems on Far Sky and New Dawn, even though he was not from that time. The

127

day progressed and they could tell when the ship left orbit around Far Sky and went into deep space. The viewports were open so they could see their progress. The cruiser Courage flew half a mile off their port side. Lia brought lunch into the ready room as the day progressed. She was clearly disturbed by the aroma of the guests, but said nothing. When Dave and Charlie finally were exhausted, Dave said, "Well, what do you think?"

"Quite a tale, Dave," Drew said at last. "If I wasn't here on this ship now, I'd think you were crazy. Maybe I'm crazy. New Dawn is all I've ever known. But I heard rumors of space travel and that we came from another planet all my life. My grandmother said she came from a place called Earth when she was a small girl. We've got piles of old equipment that doesn't work anymore. We have no idea what they were supposed to do, but there are buildings full of the stuff. You have to wonder where that came from. My wife, Corrine here, has a great grandfather who is still alive who claims to be from Earth, right honey?"

Charlie looked shocked. "We didn't think anyone from those days was still around," he replied.

Corrine held hands with her husband. She smiled and opened, "Most folks in New Dublin think he's just a crazy old man. He claims to be three hundred and ten years old. Imagine that! He says a lot of things, but who knows what's true or not."

"I'd love to meet him Corrine," Dave replied. "Do you think you can set that up for me?"

"If you are a man of your word, and let us go, I'll ask him to meet you," she said. "He's always saying how he wants to see Earth again. Do you think you could do that, Dave?"

"Yes, I can, Corrine," he replied. "In fact, we need to decide what to do with your colony as a whole. Maybe everyone should move back there for a while." Drew and Corrine looked upset. "It's an option, that's all. The Dawners need to decide for themselves what they want to do. Right now, things are bad down there, and the one thing I won't do is drop you guys off and forget about New Dawn. You are people just like us. We put you there and then abandoned you on a half-built planet. Things are only going to get worse until the whole planet reverts to its barren, dead state. I won't let that happen, even if that is what you want us to do. I hope that's clear."

"Dave, honey," Corrine said, "New Dawn is in bad shape. We can't fix it alone, we all know that. If you help us and let us build a decent home for our children and theirs, we will support you." She turned to Charlie, saying "Charlie, darling, I forgive you for kidnapping us." They all laughed.

Dave pressed a button on his panel, and said "Lia, please come in with the guards." They entered immediately.

Dave addressed the guards, "Men, Drew and Corrine are now our guests. They have agreed to respect our ship, so no weapons or shackles will be needed. Please escort them to our best guest quarters and explain how everything works. Make sure they have towels and a change of clothes." He turned to Drew and Corrine. "Please enjoy our hospitality. Rest and get cleaned up, and in two hours, Lia will come to your suite and take you on a tour of the ship. Feel free to look around, talk to anyone and ask questions about anything that comes to mind. Please ask about what Charlie and I have told you today, so you can hear it from them too. Remember we are from the twenty-first century, so we are not experts in this century, but they are. At 1800 hours, you will join Charlie and me at dinner. We will be having a welcoming feast for you both. I hope you like to drink and be merry!" Everyone hugged and left except Charlie and Dave.

Charlie smiled, widely saying, "I think that went very well, Dave."

"Pretty strong words for a kidnapper," Dave smiled. "I really hope we can turn this colony around Charlie. If we can do that, I'm beginning to think we just might found a thousand worlds."

"Two down, nine hundred and ninety-eight to go old friend," Charlie laughed as they left the room.

CHAPTER 23

Commodore Ka-a-Fa sat in the command chair of the Gallicean cruiser Dar-Fa. His ship was leading the fleet headed for Neptune in the Earth system. The fleet was one week out of Gallia and traveling at top speed. Ka-a-Fa knew his mission well. He had been personally briefed by the military High Command. He thought it was unfortunate that the great general, Fa-a-Di was not aware of the goals of the mission. The General had been a bureaucrat too long. Being High Commissioner for the Greater Gallia sphere of planets was a heavy burden for anyone, but it was not the burden of battle or leading an army. It was the burden of endless meetings and glad-handing planetary councils. It was a sorry fate for such a great military man.

Communications officer Ne-o-Ka interrupted Ka-a-Fa's train of thought. "Commodore, I have an incoming signal for you from the Chiefs of Staff," Ne-o-Ka said.

"I'll take it in my ready room," the commodore replied as he rose and walked toward a door to the left of the command chair. "Send it in here, Ne-o-Ka." The door slammed behind him.

As Ka-a-Fa sat, the view screen in front of him came to life with the images of the three top military men of Gallia. Field Marshall Je-e-Bo, Fleet Admiral Ba-a-Ka, and General Ze-u-De looked back at him. They did not appear to be happy. Ka-a-Fa said, "Gentlemen, it is a pleasure to hear from you so soon."

"Forget the pleasantries, Ka-a-Fa," Je-e-Bo replied. "These are difficult times and there is no time for that. We have just returned from meeting with the High Council. Those fools keep making our jobs more difficult."

"What happened, Je-e-Bo?" Ka-a-Fa asked.

"They have promised General Fa-a-Di the job of permanent governor for our planets in Earth's solar system," Je-e-Bo continued. "This will keep that fool in our business forever."

"If I may be permitted to say so," Ka-a-Fa said meekly, "To me, this seems like a wonderful happenstance." The three were incensed by the thought and glowered at Ka-a-Fa, but allowed him to continue. "Once the Neptune situation is resolved in our favor, Jupiter will revert to being just another new colony that will take at least two or three hundred solar cycles to develop into anything meaningful. The general will be kept busy managing construction and recruiting new settlers to move there. That will be no small task given the distance between Greater Gallia and Jupiter."

"You have an excellent point," Ba-a-Ka said. "Do you know that as part of this deal, the general's brother-in-law is to take my job as Fleet Admiral? I am over eight hundred cycles old myself, so I have been prepared for retirement for some time. Are you prepared to report to that man?"

"Lord Admiral," Fa-a-Ka said, "I attended the Gallia Prime Star Academy with Governor De-o-Nu, and I like to think of him as a close friend. He certainly doesn't have the experience to take your place, but as a way to placate Fa-a-Di, it was likely the only acceptable solution. We must also remember that having De-o-Nu under your direct control will give you a lot of leverage over Fa-a-Di. It should keep him from causing any further trouble."

General Ze-u-De rose and starting pacing about. "Those two have done so much to weaken Gallia. I would like to kill them both with my bare hands!" he growled.

Je-e-Bo laughed, saying "Ze-u-De, you are indeed an old fool. Both of them are masters of A-Nak-Fla, and could easily kill you with both hands tied behind them. "But I agree with your feelings on this. Fa-a-Di has given too much power to the outworlders. Gallia's strength is weakened every time a new military academy or university is built on another planet. He and the High Commissioners before him have bowed before the other planets and allowed those places to grow in stature to rival even Gallia. That cannot be allowed to continue."

"We must tread lightly on the issue of the outworlders, gentlemen," Ka-a-Fa cautioned. "Less than ten percent of the souls of Greater Gallia reside on the home world. Gallia cannot stand if we anger the other ninety percent of our people. I agree that Gallia needs to be preeminent in Greater Gallia, but if we make the separation too great, we risk revolution. As you may know, more than eighty percent of the crew of my fleet here are not from Gallia originally. I have tried to keep my ships' officers native Galliceans, but that was not easy. Those few cannot control the rest if they riot."

Je-e-Bo looked calmly at the other two at their table, and then at Ka-a-Fa. "Commodore, none of us wants riots or bickering within our ranks," he started. "The fate of Greater Gallia is out of all of our hands. We are all just soldiers doing a job for our people. All we can do now is focus on the mission at hand."

"Aye-aye, Field Marshall," the commodore responded.

Je-e-Bo continued, "We are all counting on you to handle the Neptune situation quickly so we can keep moving forward. With that problem gone, we hope much of the anxiety and concern within our people will diminish, and life will go back to normal. This is an enormous investment on our part. Things continue to deteriorate in the discussions with the Predaxian Alliance. We need you and your ships back on that frontier as soon as you can. Several Planetary High Commissioners have been complaining about the lack of military presence in their districts. We have even asked the Kalideans to help in those negotiations and possibly share some of their fleet for a short time. If you pull off this mission well, I can see you as Admiral Ka-a-Fa very soon. Gallia out." The view screen went blank.

Ka-a-Fa walked to his cupboard and removed a glass and a large bottle of Gallicean whisky. He poured a drink and swallowed it. He poured another and sat down behind his desk. Through his starboard viewport he could see five of his ships flying in formation. He thought about the unenviable situation he found himself in now. On the frontier, the locals loved him and his crew. They had done an admirable job controlling piracy in the area as well as limiting incursions of Predaxian ships into the region. He was doing the job of a loyal soldier. Now he was on a mission that was kept secret from the elected leader of all of Greater Gallia. General Fa-a-Di was the most respected military man in a hundred generations. Then he was elected to the High Council. Ka-a-Fa had sworn allegiance to his former teacher, and was now ignoring his rule. He muttered, "Admiral, traitor or both! How did I get such a lousy job?" A tone sounded on his control panel and he pressed a button. On his view screen was the smiling face of Fa-a-Di. "High Commissioner, what an honor to hear from you," he said, shocked by the coincidence. He took another sip of his whisky.

"Ka-a-Fa," the general said, "It is good to see your face. You must be having either a bad or exceptionally good day because I can see your whisky glass!" He raised his own glass so that the commodore could see it and laughed.

"A couple more drinks of this and I will have gone from bad to good, my friend," Ka-a-Fa responded, laughing as well.

Fa-a-Di leaned forward so his beak was almost touching the screen and whispered, "Commodore, I know exactly what you and your fleet are doing, but that's okay. We all work for the people of Greater Gallia and must follow our orders."

Ka-a-Fa looked stunned, and stuttered, "That is absolutely true General." He took another long drink and went to the cupboard to refill his glass.

"Ka-a-Fa," Fa-a-Di began, "Don't be worried. I won't stand in the way of your mission to Neptune. At least not yet. As you should know by now, we are working with scientists from Earth and Kalidus to understand the mental images the Neptunians are sending. I think it is doubtful that we will succeed before your arrival. But I believe that God will help us learn at the appropriate time. If your fleet arrives and destroys those creatures before we learn what they are saying, then that was their fate. If they are destined to survive, we will learn first and stop the bloodshed before it starts."

"God willing, you will succeed, General," the commodore responded.

"God willing, indeed Ka-a-Fa," Fa-a-Di continued. "I love you like a brother, Ka-a-Fa. I hope you know that. You were one of my best students at the academy and at my A-Nak-Fla camp at Ze-e-Akla. You were even best man when De-o-Nu married my sister. But I will tell you this now. If we are beginning to understand the Neptunians and have reason to believe they are not dangerous, and you choose to attack anyway, my fleet will attack you. I would never want to hurt you, son, but you and your crew would die in that battle. Many of our troops are fiercely loyal to me. I am the only one who encouraged the development of military academies off of Gallia. I am the one who gave high government and military positions to people from the other worlds. Those outworlders as some call them are the vast majority of our citizens. It is long past time for Gallia to share the spotlight with them."

"Fa-a-Di," the commodore said, "you know I would rather be on the Predaxian frontier right now fighting the real fight. This political gamesmanship is getting totally out of hand. But I do have my orders."

"Ka-a-Fa, my son," he replied. "I know, and I fully expect you to carry them out. I would personally have you court-martialed if you did not. However, those orders are to eliminate a threat from the Neptunians. If they are not a threat, will you attack anyway because those old fools on Gallia tell you to? Don't answer now. You probably don't know what you would do, and that's great. It means you have time to think about it and come to the correct decision. To help you think, I want to tell you a few things. First, I know the Earth warships are little threat to you. But they are positioning ten cruisers to be ready in case of a conflict. If you attack them, it would be a galactic incident of monumental proportions. The Kalideans will not be sending any ships to the Predaxian frontier. The ships they promised to send are going to Neptune to join our forces. Finally, you know I have a few crews fiercely loyal to me who will do as I say. I am hoping to have twenty cruisers around Jupiter by the time you arrive."

"Yes General," Ka-a-Fa stammered, "I understand you are a very powerful adversary. I would never wish to confront you." He drained his glass. "Fa-a-Di, I have faith this will unfold in the proper way. I do not wish to die in a Gallicean civil war."

"Ka-a-Fa," the general said, "I believe all will work out too. But before I go, I want to share one last thought with you." Ka-a-Fa was staring blanking out his viewport as the general continued,

"Of those twenty loyal crews who will fight with me if needed, six are in your own fleet right now." Fa-a-Di snorted.

"You are bluffing General," he replied. "I hand picked my crews. Their allegiance is to me first and Gallia second."

"Perhaps I am bluffing, Ka-a-Fa. In the moment you decide to attack harmless life on Neptune, you will find the old general has many friends. You don't have to believe me now, but you will believe me then! Jupiter out," Fa-a-Di laughed as the screen went blank.

Ka-a-Fa sat quietly for several minutes. He tried to imagine which of his personally selected captains would switch sides in battle. He thought about the Chiefs of Staff and their demands and how they were only interested in maintaining and growing their own power. He worried about the citizens in the Predaxian region who were now unprotected. He thought about High Commissioner Fa-a-di. His studies under the general had been the happiest time of his life. He thought about the Neptunians too. Were they really scheming to take over Greater Gallia, or were the fear-mongers just fools? He decided he was thinking too much and returned to the bridge.

As the door closed behind him, the crystal spider in the upper corner of the room moved. He unfurled its wings and landed next to the whisky bottle that Ka-a-Fa had left open. It extended a slender tendril down into the bottle and took a long drink. After withdrawing the tendril, it glowed bright white, and disappeared.

CHAPTER 24

Dave Brewster was getting very nervous. The Ticonderoga has been orbiting New Dawn for two weeks now. Drew and Corrine Baker had been returned to their city as promised. The two colony ships were continuously shuttling down supplies to the colonists. There had been no further attacks on his crew, but little else good was happening. Drew had arranged for a meeting of the New Dawn High Council in New Dublin. It took more than a week for the representatives to travel to the city. Dave had offered the ship's shuttle fleet to expedite travel, but only a few of the farthest settlements took them up on the offer. Clearly, the Dawners were not yet comfortable with the intrusion into their everyday lives.

Dave was sitting in the main dining room on board sipping his espresso. Things were moving so slowly that he needed the kick from espresso to keep him from dropping off to sleep. He had recurring dreams about flying around that blue planet with the flying globes of light. When he thought the memory might be fading, he would have the dream again and be right back there, battling the star cruiser with no weapons. The less sleep the better, he thought. Charlie and Aria entered the dining room and Charlie joined Dave at the table. Aria went to the counter to order for them. "Good morning, Charlie, how are you two today?" Dave said.

"Going crazy just like you, pal," Charlie said. "This waiting for the Dawners to make a decision is driving me crazy. I heard a major sandstorm is headed toward New Dublin. That will likely cut off communications for a few days. More delay."

Aria joined them at the table. On her tray were three cappuccinos and a large plate of pastries. "Dave, please help yourself," she said. "How is Darlene? Where is she anyway?" She took a cup of coffee and a chocolate croissant and nibbled it.

"She is with the High Commissioner and a contingent from Kalidus holding negotiations on Gallia," Dave answered. "Apparently we have a situation brewing. At least that's what she can tell me."

"That is odd. I had a talk with Fa-a-Di who is on Jupiter just a while ago," Charlie said. "You'd think he would be on Gallia negotiating for his people."

"The times are changing on Gallia, Charlie," Dave replied. "Fa-a-Di is near the end of his second term as High Commissioner, and has decided not to run for reelection. I can't say that I blame him either. Politics is not a game many can play well. It's just like this situation on New Dawn. I can't believe it is taking this long!"

Aria reached out and touched Dave's hand. "Dave, these people are making decisions that will change their lives forever. They know their way of life is not sustainable. All they need is the time to agree that things need to change and to believe that we really want to help," she said soothingly.

Dave held her hand for a moment and then released it. "Aria, I know you are right about that. I know that it's true in my heart as well. There are just too many things going on now, and time is short."

"Dave, I know the Courage was summoned back to Earth this morning," Charlie added. "I'm a bit concerned our colony ships have no protection. I know there are no known pirates in this area, but it does make me nervous nonetheless. Besides, what's going on back home that needs so much protection?"

"I've asked for ten star fighters to be sent here as soon as possible," Dave answered. I think five of them are due to jump to Far Sky today. "But I agree something is happening that is being hidden. I don't like it at all. It's almost enough to make one jump back to the unemployment line in the twenty-first." They all laughed. They sat back, enjoying their breakfast and mutual company. Dave remembered when he first met Aria. He had thought she was so beautiful and unique looking. Now, looking around the room, it was Charlie and he who were unique. "Charlie, tell me about you and Lia?" he said at last.

Charlie laughed and looked at Aria who was smiling broadly. "Lia is my daughter, Dave, if that's what you're asking. It's a bit of a long story, but since we are at the whim of the Dawners, I guess I have time, if it's okay with you, Aria?" She smiled and nodded. "Time travel can be very confusing, Dave, if you haven't already figured that out. When I first moved to San Diego, after my divorce and quitting my job, I was a bit of a bum. Actually, I had a lot of money, but with no connections, I just wandered about taking notes and getting to know the people around town. It was a lot of fun, but not very fulfilling as a replacement occupation. That was when I first started hanging out at coffee shops with my laptop, listening to conversations and dreaming up concepts for my books. This was all about ten years before I met you Dave. One day I was headed to the shop first thing in the morning when a blinding flash of light hit me. I thought a car had flashed his high beams or something. I felt very woozy after that and sat on the curb where I had been standing. Someone touched me on the shoulder and I turned to see a very unique looking and beautiful woman. She asked me if I was okay and offered to buy me a coffee. That woman was Lyra Lawson, Lia's mother to be." Charlie took a sip of his cappuccino and a bit of pastry.

Dave heard a tone on his earpiece and touched the contact. He listened carefully, acknowledged the message and closed the connection. "Charlie, you can continue your story on the shuttle. Drew said they are ready to meet with us. A shuttle craft is standing by in the shuttle bay. Let's go." The three hurried out the door and into the hallway. The shuttle bay was at the bottom of the ship and so they took a lift down. They walked down another hallway and came to the shuttle bay. The shuttle pilot led them to the small ship. The shuttles were designed to carry up to one hundred people back and forth from a planet or another ship. The seats could be easily removed to make room for large amounts of cargo. This shuttle had two banks of seats to accommodate up to ten people. For this trip, it was only Dave, Charlie, Aria and Lia, who was already strapped in when they arrived.

Dave signaled the pilot that they were ready to leave. The ship pulled out of the shuttle bay and into space. The Ticonderoga loomed above them like a giant mountain of steel, gleaming in the reflected light from the surface of New Dawn. Below them was the vast expanse of the planet's surface. Dave could see the outline of the sandstorm that was approaching New Dublin. It was still a day or two away, and he hoped he would be back on board before that monster hit. "Okay, Charlie, on with the story, if you can," he said.

"Lia's story, you mean," Charlie corrected him. He looked at his daughter who was blushing. Aria put her arm around Lia's shoulders and squeezed her. "Lyra was so sweet that day, and being newly single again, I was easily overcome by her beauty and kindness. I think you could say I was overwhelmed that such a young, beautiful girl would be so impressed with me. Before I finished my coffee, I had completely forgotten the bright flash and my wooziness. We dated for several months. She told me she was an anthropologist, but it never entered my mind she was from the future. In my job, I'd been around the world a number of times, and seen so many different races of people, I just assumed she was a mix or from somewhere I hadn't been yet. After six or seven months, I was getting up the courage to ask her to marry me. I arranged a special dinner at the Marine Room and met her there. We had a wonderful time, watching the waves crash against the glass, holding hands and loving each other's company. It was perfect. When I thought the time was right, I pulled an engagement ring from my pocket, dropped to one knee and asked her to marry me," Charlie remembered. The shuttle craft shuddered as it hit the denser atmosphere nearer the surface. They were flying over the New Dublin Lake which stretched for hundreds of miles in each direction. New Dublin was approaching slowly in the distance. "Lyra's reaction was not what I expected. She started crying. I thought I really screwed this up now, and I guess I did. She told me that she couldn't marry me, and that I would never understand why. She took my hand, squeezed it, said good-bye, and left."

"Wow," Dave said, "that was pretty harsh. I admit the thought of marrying you is pretty scary, but running out?"

"Thanks for the vote of confidence, Admiral," Charlie continued. "I didn't find out until much later that Lyra had found she was pregnant, and reported it to the Chief Engineer at the time. I don't even remember what his name was. She was reprimanded for getting involved with a local and ordered to return immediately. I never saw her again."

"Don't worry about my mom, Dave," Lia began. "She is now governor of Day's End, where I was born seventy two years ago. When she was booted out of Temporal Command, she took a job as a terraforming expert for the colony. Over the years, she moved up the ranks, got elected to the planetary council, and now runs the whole show. She never knew Dad would be in our time. She moved on. Even though it's only been ten years for Dad, it's been much longer for her." She held Charlie's hand tightly. "And look how great I turned out!" They all laughed. The sun was directly overhead as the shuttle set down in a newly built shuttle pad near the town center. They all removed their restraints and headed out into the midday heat.

Summer was the dry season in New Dublin. The temperature was around ninety degrees, with virtually zero humidity. The thin atmosphere made the sun feel even hotter. They hurried across the town square to the newly constructed Council Hall. They entered and were relieved by the air conditioning his crew had recently installed. Corrine Baker was waiting for them. She led them to the Council Chamber and offered them seats in the middle of the room. Around them sat the representatives from the forty population centers on high benches.

A very thin man stood and banged his gavel. He seemed to be about eighty years old in Dave's time. He was unshaven and his hair was unkempt. "Admiral Brewster and other honored guests," he began, "I am Adam Farso, representing the city of New Baltimore, and her five hundred souls. Today, I have been elected High Commissioner for the High Council of New Dawn. I welcome you to our home." All the councilors stood and applauded. Dave rose and went to shake his hand, which was dry and thin, but very strong. He waved Dave back to his seat. "We have taken a vote on whether we should accept your help, and by a vote of thirty ayes, seven nays, and three abstentions, we agree to rejoin the High Council for Humanity. Meeting adjourned." He slammed his gavel down. "Now, please join us in the antechamber for a cocktail reception." More applause rang out. The entire group moved out of the chambers. All the councilors came to meet Dave and his crew. Handshakes and hugs were the order of the day.

Dave was ecstatic. New Dawn was going to be saved. He was very happy to meet and talk to each of the councilors and learn about their towns or cities and tell them his story. His crew had made preparations and brought down a large supply of champagne and other drinks. The Dawners offered their food and local drink, which was colorless and very strong. It was going to be a great day. He could now focus all of his attention on the Neptune situation. Just like New Dawn, he felt new confidence that there would not be a war with the Galliceans. Charlie, Aria and Lia were also enjoying themselves very much. Everyone was in a great mood, except Corrine Baker.

She came up to Dave and tapped him on the shoulder, asking him to step outside for a moment. When they were away from everyone else, she whispered "Dave, you remember about my great grandfather?"

"Of course, Corrine," he replied. "And I will follow through on that too. When can I see him?"

"That's kind of the problem Dave," she said. "He's disappeared again. When Drew and I told him about what happened on your ship, he was very excited to see Earth again. He started retelling the old stories about how he came here two hundred years ago with his wife and two daughters, one of whom was my grand-mother. We had a couple of drinks together and said our good nights. In the morning he was gone. He left a note saying he couldn't leave here without Jake and was going off to his secret place to get him."

"Is that close to here? Who is Jake anyway?" Dave asked.

"It's about a day's drive. I think I know the way. I was going to go there now, but thought you might want to go along. You see, Jake is his imaginary friend. We told you some people think my great grandfather is crazy. He had told us for years and years about Jake. It's a little scary. He's an old man, and he's entitled to any friends he wants, real or imaginary. With the sandstorm headed this way, I've got to leave now. Do you want to join me or not?"

Dave considered, and said, "We could take my shuttle and get there quicker."

"Won't work, Dave," she replied. "I'm used to seeing the landmarks as I drive along the ground. It won't be the same up in the air. I don't want him alone out there in the storm. He says that blue flashing, winged glass spider will keep him safe, but it's only in his head."

Dave's mind was reeling. He thought again about the recurring dream. Those glowing creatures flying with him over the blue planet did look like spiders, he was almost certain. "Wait here, Corrine," he started, "I'll go tell Charlie what we're doing. Then I'll be ready to go. Within a minute, he met Corrine outside and climbed into her vehicle, which was more like a heavily armored truck. They sped down the main road through town and out into the barren countryside with the large sandstorm looming in the distance ahead of them.

CHAPTER 25

Dave was wishing he had reconsidered Charlie's offer to take his place on the trip. Corrine was very intensely focused on the road ahead. After two hours on the main highway, she had turned off onto what was just a path through the dirt. As they wound their way into the hills, the surface got rougher and she was forced to slow down. He was grateful for that. "It's not safe to go too slow around here, Dave," she said. "The further we get from the city, the higher the chance of running into bandits."

"Bandits," Dave repeated.

"Life on New Dawn is rough," she replied. "Many folks can't stomach town life. There are too many rules and not enough money to go around. The meager existence we live today is only possible due to sharing goods from town to town. New Dublin has the most fresh water, and that's one of our largest exports, along with fish. The soil is no good for a lot of crops, so we import those from other towns. Then there are the towns along our one ocean, like New London. We get our salt and seafood from there."

"And the bandits prey on the truckers. That's why this truck is so heavily armed," Dave said. He heard a metallic plinking sound.

"That's small arms fire, Dave," Corrine replied before he could ask. "That happens all the time. The fact that I'm the head of the police and they know it makes me a convenient target. The main things I look for are land mines. Even this behemoth won't do well if we hit one. I'm pulling off road to avoid that." The ride went from bad to horrible as they headed off road. Dave wondered if he could survive much more of the shaking. They crossed over a hill and a large fertile valley lay before them. Along the edge of the valley was a large river flowing slowly in the direction of New Dublin Lake and a long, straight stretch of concrete highway. "That's the road to New Baltimore, where High Commissioner Farso is from. It is the bread basket of New Dawn. Most of the crops on the planet are grown in this region. A lot prettier than New Dublin, isn't it?"

It was. The valley stretched as far as the eye could see in either direction. Much of the land was fallow, but farms were scattered about, each with a large heavy fence around the buildings. Dave knew this was part of the planet that was terraformed. The conditions were just too ideal to exist this close to the barrenness of New Dublin. "Corrine, are we going to the valley? Is that where your great grandfather's secret place is?" he asked.

"No, Dave," she replied. "New Baltimore isn't very secret. But don't worry, we are almost there." She turned up the side of a second hill. The climb was very steep and even bumpier. Near the summit, there was a large cut into the hillside that was not visible from the surrounding area. She pulled her truck into that cut. Dave could see a small piece of pavement next to the cut where a steel door was concealed. A small armored vehicle sat parked there. "We made it, Dave," Corrine said as she pulled alongside the other vehicle and turned hers off. "Keep an eye out Dave, this is not a safe place." She pulled a revolver from her holster and stepped out of the vehicle, looking around carefully. Dave climbed out and crossed in front of the truck near the door. Corrine moved to the door and pressed a hidden switch, saying, "Great Grandpa, it's Corrine, let us in." He heard a mechanism moving in the door. Dave felt a sharp pain in his right arm and then heard a pop. He looked down to see blood soaking his uniform, and looked up at her. "Dave, you've been shot," she said as he fell to the ground unconscious.

Dave was flying again over the blue planet. This time the dream was different. He remembered being shot and looked at his arm. The sleeve was still blood-soaked, but he saw that one of the flying creatures had extended a slender tendril and was touching the spot where he was hit. The pain went away, and he could see the blood disappearing from his uniform. Even the hole in the garment was mended. He looked at the creature and thought he could see it smile at him. It was glowing very bright blue. He tried to say thank you, but no words came out. In his mind, he heard a calm voice saying, "You are quite welcome, Dave Brewster."

He suddenly awoke to find himself inside Corrine's great grandfather's secret place. The place was a storage bunker built to store terraforming supplies. His crews had recently built several hundred such depots on Far Sky. The room was very large, almost one hundred meters long by fifty meters wide. Mountains of unused equipment surrounded them. He looked at his arm, which seemed to be healed, although the sleeve was still covered in dried blood. He felt remarkably good for a man who had just been shot. He sat up and could see Corrine asleep on an improvised bed. A few meters further, he could see the old man working in a makeshift kitchen. Dave cleared his throat and offered a weak "Hello."

The man smiled broadly, grabbed two cups and filled them with fresh coffee. He strode over to Dave's bed, extending his hand. "Admiral Brewster, I'm glad to see you back with us. I'm Corrine's great grandfather, Horace Hildebrand. How are you feeling today?"

Dave smiled and gladly accepted the cup of coffee. He took a sip and found it to be excellent. "I feel fine, Horace, especially with this great coffee. I am grateful to you or Corrine for mending my arm so quickly. How long was I asleep?"

Horace pulled up a chair and sat next to Dave. "Three days, Son. I'm not surprised, you needed the rest to recoup the blood you lost," Horace replied. "And you don't owe us any gratitude Dave. It was Jake who fixed you up."

"Jake, but Corrine told me . . ." Dave started.

"Oh, don't listen to her and those other folks in town," Horace scoffed. "Look at your arm, young man. Do you see any scars or sutures or anything?" Dave looked and saw only his own smooth skin. "You know what it's like on New Dawn. Do you think we could do anything like that?"

"So, Jake is real," Dave asked. "Can I meet him? Is he here?"

"Oh, he's here alright, but he's kind of shy," Horace said as he looked about. "I talked to him about you and your ships coming to help us. He was very happy. I told him I wanted him to go to Earth with me. He wasn't too sure about that though. He did ask is he might be able to use some of your equipment to help him get home. I think he called it a portal, or portage, something like that."

Corrine had heard some of the discussion and came to join the men. "You still telling stories about Jake, Great Grandpa?" she asked.

"Corrine Honey, look at the man's arm! It's completely healed," Horace insisted. She looked at Dave's arm and was amazed that the injury was gone. "Did you do that? Do you think I could have done it? Certainly you don't think Dave fixed himself?"

Corrine looked very concerned. "Dave, when we got you inside, we did what we could to stop the bleeding. That I remember. He said he had some remedies he had found here in the bunker that

150

might hold you until we could signal your ship. Once you were stable, I was so exhausted I had to sleep. I guess I've been sleeping a couple of days now." She turned to her relative, held his hand and gently said, "Okay Great Grandpa, let's say that Jake is real and he did this. Why don't you ask him to come out and meet us?"

Horace pulled his hand away, stood and started pacing. He ranted, "I don't know if I will or not. You don't believe me. Your family thinks I'm crazy. You'll just make fun of Jake and me."

Dave stood and walked up to Horace, looked him in the eyes and said, "Horace, I believe you. I have been having dreams about a blue planet full of creatures like Jake. I thought it was a random dream, but they keep coming back. In each dream, I am flying with thousands of the glass spiders over a blue planet. A space ship is attacking their city and they try to fight back, and I go with them. The ship turns its fire on us and we have no defenses. As I slept after being shot, I had the dream again. Only this time, I remembered my arm and looked, and one of the spiders was healing me. I could hear it talking directly into my brain and I understood what it said. I think the spider in my dream was Jake. If there is one of those creatures who can communicate with us, it can save their whole planet and prevent a possible galactic war. We've got to get back to my ship."

Corrine had sat down on Dave's bed and was shaking her head bewildered by what Dave had just said. She said, "Wow, Dave. Now I'm beginning to think you two are sane and I'm the crazy one. But we're not going anywhere now. We are in the middle of the sandstorm. It will likely take another day or two to pass. There is nothing to do but sit and wait." She walked over to Horace and threw her arms around him. "I'm sorry for not believing you Great Grandpa. Can you forgive me?"

He hugged her close to him. "There's nothing to forgive, Honey. Half of the time I thought I had gone crazy too." He looked around the room and shouted, "Jake, we've got company. Admiral Dave is here to take you home. Come on out now." A few moments passed and a flicker of blue light caught their eyes at the far end of the room. The glasslike creature floated through the air on its gossamer wings and landed on the table in the kitchen area. Horace said, "When Jake likes to talk we need to sit close to him. He'll touch us with his little arms and can speak directly into our minds." The three took seats at the table. Three slender tendrils rose from Jake's body and one touched each of the three.

"Hello Dave and Corrine," it thought to them. "Horace likes to call me Jake because it's simpler and more human. My name is Jacomofledes Benomafolays and I am from the planet No-Makla, which I believe the people on your home world call Neptune."

"Jacomofledes," Dave said aloud, "I can see now why Horace calls you Jake. First let me thank you for healing me. More importantly, I think your home world is in big trouble. I want to help you and prevent a galactic war."

"Dave," the thoughts came through again, "you are quite welcome. I have sensed danger for No-Makla. Like Horace and Corrine, I am stranded here. We maklans are normally able to make space and temporal jumps without a portal, but I am too far away to jump without other maklans. What can we do together to stop this tragedy?"

CHAPTER 26

The sandstorm lasted two more days. Dave and Jake were able to get the air conditioning and water treatment systems running. They also turned on the exterior sensors, which did not work well with the storm overhead. Dave told Jake the whole story about the possible Gallicean attack on No-Makla. Jake was certain he could warn his planet if he were able to use a portal to jump back to the Earth solar system after the storm cleared.

On the last day of the storm, Jake told Horace, Corrine and Dave about the history of his race. The maklans were an ancient race, older than many of the stars in the galaxy. Their home world, named Ai-Makla, was destroyed when their sun became a nova more than one billion Earth years ago. Two hundred thousand years before that, they developed the technology to calculate when their star would die. There was global panic when they learned how little time was left. All of the planetary resources were reallocated to focus on moving the population to other star systems. Stars were too distant to reach by traditional space flight, so they had to find a better way. It took them one hundred thousand years to develop space jump technology. A massive portal was created in orbit over Ai-Makla. It was used to launch smaller portals near planets in neighboring systems. Smaller ships jumped through those portals to examine planets for suitability to maklan life. Eventually, over ten thousand portals were built and spread out through the galaxy. The portal near Io was put there by the maklans a billion Earth years ago. It was the last portal to be built.

Dave had always assumed that humanity or perhaps the Kalideans had built those portals. Eventually, the maklans found five hundred suitable systems, including the Earth system. Thousands of colony ships were launched through the portals to bring the maklans to their new homes. In the last ten thousand years before the Ai-Makla nova, temperatures started rising dramatically on the home world. The sun was becoming more unstable, with large gamma ray pulses shooting through space. There was widespread damage on Ai-Makla and in orbit about it by those pulses. The portal was moved to the side of the planet away from the sun to protect it. The colony ships were on their own in their new solar systems. Maklans were fleeing Ai-Makla as quickly as possible. Soon, there was virtually no governmental infrastructure as the cities emptied out. Jake said his ancestor was on one of the last colony ships that jumped to Io before the nova. Legend said that all maklans through the galaxy looked to the Ai-Makla sun on the date and time when their sun was supposed to die. The nova was very bright and looked like a second sun for several weeks before it faded into a nebula. Each year that day is remembered as the Great Rebirth.

Dave asked Jake if the different maklan planets had any communication among them. He told them some did at first, but over the generations, the great distances made it more difficult to connect, and most became isolated. Jake told them about one colony that moved to a more Earth-like world on the opposite side of what is now Greater Gallia. Over the millennia, those maklans devolved into more animal like creatures and were no longer able to fly or communicate telepathically. The rumors on No-Makla were that those creatures had become warlike and their telepathic ability had morphed into the ability to control other creature's minds. He said their new home world was called Predax, and they had gained control over several other planets by controlling the minds of their leaders. They were to be avoided at all costs.

Jake told them his species had lived in Earth's solar system for a billion years. From the original ten million souls that jumped from Ai-Makla, there were now forty billion maklans living on Neptune, and another one hundred million on Uranus. Fewer maklans chose Uranus due to its tilted axis, which made one side face the sun continually. It was always day or night there, depending on which hemisphere one would live. Most of the residents lived along the equator where the slight axis tilt away from ninety degrees allowed for some normalcy. There had been colonies on all of the planets from time to time, except Mercury and Venus, which were too inhospitable. When they discovered life blooming on Earth, they closed the colonies there and relocated their people to Mars. The colony on Mars was the largest in the system between one billion and five hundred million years ago. Over time, the atmosphere was thinning due to the small planet size. That led to increasing radiation from the sun. Those colonies were then abandoned, and virtually all maklans moved to Neptune. They chose not to develop Jupiter or Saturn for the same reason they abandoned Earth. They did not want to interfere with the indigenous life.

About one million years ago, the great maklan scientist, Arinofalez Zionaster developed the tools to allow maklans to jump through space or time without a portal. All maklans were implanted with the device to enable space jumping at birth. Temporal jumping was tightly restricted, due to the risk of distorting the time continuum. Any trained individual could jump to any planet in the solar system. If they formed a circle of ten or more, the group could jump up to twenty light years. That was why Jake was trapped here with the rest of the Dawners. He needed a portal or more maklans to get back home.

On the evening of the last night of the storm, Corrine and Horace made a feast for Dave and Jake. Dave had found a case of Scotch whisky from Earth buried among the supplies, and opened a couple of bottles to go with the food. They all sat together laughing and enjoying each other's company, grateful to be getting out of that room when the storm cleared sometime during the night. Jake had his tendrils touching the others so that he could speak with them. He knew he needed to eat, but the human food was not appetizing. He extended another tendril into one of the Scotch bottles and tasted it. "Dave, this whisky is great!" Jake exclaimed, "I've never tasted anything like this before. You said this is a fermented mash from a place called Scotland on your home world?"

Dave was feeling the heat in his face from the drink as well. "Jake, this is some of the best hooch my planet has to offer. Let's all have another drink!" he replied.

"Hey guys," Jake slurred into their minds, "Let me try something." He withdrew his tendrils from the others. "Can you hear me?" he asked.

Dave said, "Yes, I hear you Jake." The others said they could hear him too. "This is great. How did that happen?"

"Dave, we've spent a lot of time connected to each other over the past couple of days," Jake began. "I'm thinking that our link has become strong enough that I don't need the tendrils anymore. I don't know over what distance we can communicate, but I can't wait to find out." They all laughed and drank more, until the second bottle was empty. Everyone was too tired and drunk to clean up after the meal. They all went to their respective beds and collapsed.

Dave was having a terrible night. Too much food and drink made him uneasy and he tossed and turned for what seemed like hours before falling asleep. He felt like he had been sleeping for only a minute when he heard Jake's voice in his head. "Dave, it's Jake. Please wake up," the voice said. Dave opened his eyes and looked around the dark room. He could not see Jake anywhere. He looked at his watch and it read 0700 hours. He had been sleeping seven hours, but needed a lot more. "Dave, wake up!" Jake shouted into his brain.

Dave thought, "Okay, Jake, I'm awake. Where are you?"

Jake thought, "Dave, I'm on your ship, the Ticonderoga. When the storm cleared, I could sense fifteen other maklans on your ship. I talked to them and they helped me jump up here. We are all going to jump back to No-Makla. There are enough of us to do that now."

"Jake," Dave thought, "I need you to go to Io with me. I told you that we need to find a way to open communications between the maklans and the Galliceans. You are the key, Jake. You've already figured out how to talk to humans. You can work with my son, Bill and his team to get this thing done on time. Don't let me down, Jake!"

"Dave," Jake said, "I will be there in three or four Earth days at the very latest. You told me the Gallicean fleet might attack my planet. I need to check on my family and talk to our High Council and get things moving. Dave, I haven't seen my wife in over two hundred years. Give me those few days. It will take you most of one day to get to Far Sky to be able to jump to Io yourself. Have faith, friend, I will be there."

"Okay Jake. I trust you. You did save my life after I was shot. I owe you this and a lot more," Dave replied.

"Thanks Dave," Jake said. "I will be there. I've already been talking to the team on your ship about the situation, and we're getting lots of good ideas. Dave, we're jumping in a few seconds. You won't be able to communicate with me from twenty light years away. Hopefully, when you get to Io, I can reach you telepathically. Thanks for rescuing me from Horace and giving us time to stop this war."

Dave rolled over listening to the pounding in his head. A tone sounded in his earpiece. "Dave, where the heck have you been," Charlie said. "We've been going crazy since we lost contact with you up here. Are you okay? We're reading your signal and you are a hundred miles from New Dublin. Should we send a shuttle?"

Dave smiled and said, "Charlie, I could sure use a coffee right about now. Too much Scotch last night. I am fine and am with Corrine Baker and her great grandfather, Horace Hildebrand. His secret place is an old terraforming supply dump. There are lots of good supplies we can use down here. Send two shuttles to my coordinates, and be sure to send armed guards. There are lots of bandits down here. I was even shot by one."

"Are you okay, Dave? Did someone take out the bullet?" Charlie asked.

"I'm fine now Charlie," he replied. "But you won't believe it. The answer to all my problems showed up here, cured my arm, and will likely bring peace to the galaxy for the next thousand years."

"Are you still drunk, man?" Charlie asked.

"No, but I am hung over," Dave said. "Please get those shuttles on the way soon, and ask someone to bring me a cappuccino and chocolate croissant."

Charlie laughed. "I'll bring it myself Admiral!"

CHAPTER 27

The Dar-Fa and her fleet had been traveling for weeks in the void between Gallicean and human space and now found themselves approaching the edge of human controlled region. Ka-a-Fa was not looking forward to this. The Chiefs of Staff had not given him any advice on how to convince the humans that his ten star cruisers were just on a pleasure trip and needed access to the Earth star system. Any time now, the humans would identify their approach and hail them.

As if on cue, Ne-o-Ka, the communications officer said, "Commodore, I have an incoming signal from the human star cruiser Resolute. Should I put it on speaker?'

"Yes, Ne-o-Ka, let's hear what they have to say," he replied.

The translated human voice said, "Greetings Gallicean fleet. I am Captain Willow Westerman of the Resolute. As you are no doubt aware, your ships are on a course to enter our space in the next half hour. What is the nature of your business in this region?"

The bridge crew all looked at the commodore, wondering what he would say. He was wondering the same thing. He sat quietly for a moment, and then began, "Captain Westerman, I am Commodore Ka-a-Fa of the Gallicean fleet. We are on a mission to patrol the planets in the Earth star system that your gracious civilization has granted to us. Our great general, Fa-a-Di has requested that we bring a large contingent of scientific specialists and their equipment to expedite our exploration. The ships in my fleet were the only ones available for this mission."

"Aye-aye, Commodore. Please refrain from entering our space until I am able to confirm your orders," Captain Westerman replied.

"Helmsman," Ka-a-Fa began, "Tell the fleet to turn to a heading parallel to the human frontier and reduce speed to one-quarter until we hear back from their ship. I am not ready to start a war with the humans just yet." Ka-a-Fa rose from his seat and paced about the bridge. There was no one who would verify that mission. He had just made it up. He was certain he would face a court-martial now, either at the hands of the Chiefs of Staff or Fa-a-Di himself. It was a risky move to bring the general into the mix, but he could not think of another answer. He sat heavily, nervously awaiting the response. Time seemed to freeze, and Ka-a-Fa thought he might sit here forever waiting.

After five minutes, the image of Willow Westerman on the bridge of the Resolute appeared on the Dar-Fa's view screen, saying, "Commodore, we have verified your mission with General Fa-a-Di himself. He offers his greetings and hopes the rest of your flight is safe. You have our approval to enter our space and proceed to Jupiter in the Earth system. Good day, sir." Willow was smiling.

"Thank you very much, Captain," Ka-a-Fa replied. "Your gracious words are appreciated, and show the value of our cooperation. Be well, Dar-Fa out." The screen went blank and was replaced by the view of space in front of the ship. "Ne-o-Ka, tell the fleet to resume our original course and speed. Also, ask Captain No-a-Je of the Bak-Lar to jump over here and meet me in my ready room as soon as possible." Ka-a-Fa rose to leave the bridge. "And tell the supply depot to send five bottles of whisky to me as soon as possible."

Chapter 27

"Aye-aye, Commodore," he replied as Ka-a-Fa disappeared into his ready room.

The commodore slumped into his chair in the ready room. He was frantic that Fa-a-Di would have personally authorized the fleet to enter human space. If the general had just said no, the entire mission would have failed. Ka-a-Fa would have been disgraced in front of all Greater Gallia. He probably would have been fired or at least reduced in rank.

As he sat brooding, a crew member hastily entered with the bottles of whisky. He was quickly followed by Captain No-a-Je who took one of the bottles and two glasses and sat across from the commodore. No-a-Je opened the bottle and filled the two glasses, making certain that the commodore's glass had more whisky. He took a sip and said, "Commodore, let's have a toast to the success of our mission!"

Ka-a-Fa touched his glass to the other and drank half. "No-a-Je," he started, "I've known you my whole life, right?"

"Yes, Ka-a-Fa," the captain replied, "We grew up together and went to the same schools. The only time we were separated was when we were assigned to different ships. What's wrong, Brother?"

"No-a-Je, this mission is tearing me apart. You know the tension between the Chiefs of Staff and Fa-a-Di. There is too much hatred and mistrust there, don't you think?" he asked.

The captain downed his drink and rose, pacing about the room. "Yes I do, Brother. Most of the crews in our fleet are constantly gossiping about the situation on Gallia. Fifty years ago, when the Predaxian War started, it was those four military men who turned the tide of battle and kept Gallia from being invaded by the enemy. The way that Fa-a-Di and Je-e-Bo led the attack on the Alliance fleet at Nok-lak-a is the subject of hundreds of military textbooks. Now, they behave like mortal enemies," No-a-Je said.

Ka-a-Fa pounded his fist on his desk and replied, "That's exactly what I'm talking about, Brother! I've heard the stories how Fa-a-Di is trying to give too much power to the outworlders and the Chiefs are vehemently against that, but it doesn't make sense. How can the small population of Gallia expect to keep all the power?"

"On my ship," the captain whispered, "we have demanded no one use that word. All the citizens of Greater Gallia are equal. Calling the majority outworlders is very insulting."

"I agree Brother," Ka-a-Fa replied. "For some reason though, the Chiefs have no problem brandishing around words like that. Now we are supposed to go to Neptune and risk a war with the humans and Kalideans in order to eliminate a threat that may not even exist. It's crazy!" The commodore poured another drink, sat back and sipped it.

"Well Brother, we don't know that the Neptunians are not a threat either," No-a-Je said. "There is still a chance those creatures will attack us. After all, weren't their mental signals hurting our crews in orbit?"

"True," the commodore responded. "I am certain that is why Fa-a-Di approved our entry into human space. If he denied us, and the Neptunians are determined to be a danger, then his career is over. He could be indicted for aiding and abetting the enemy. It's better to have us there just in case."

"My concern, Brother is that the Neptunians are not a threat and the Chiefs may order us to destroy them anyway," No-a-Je said. "Then what will we do?"

"That is the question of the day, Brother. If I had to answer right now, I am one hundred percent certain we will be ordered to attack no matter what." Ka-a-Fa closed his eyes and dropped his head into his hands. He lifted his head after a moment and stared at No-a-Je, saying, "Brother, in that moment when I am forced to order the attack, what will you and my other captains do?"

No-a-Je took a long drink, set the glass down and stared into space for a minute. He looked at his lifelong friend and replied, "Brother, a soldier must follow orders. But a man has beliefs he must live with. Right now, I don't know the answer. I think I would follow you to our mutual death if that is what we are ordered to do. If the Alliance attacked today, I would gladly give my life to defeat them. If the Neptunians are a threat, I will kill each of them with my bare hands and beak. If we know they are not dangerous, I just don't know. A million years ago, when Gallia was a conqueror of worlds, life was simpler. Our ancestors would follow orders and ask questions later. Now we live in a peaceful land of laws and treaties. Asking us to revert to those old ways is not a fair question. What will you do, Brother?"

"First, I would drink at least one bottle of this whisky," Ka-a-Fa said as he drained his glass again. "Then, I would think about my family, my friends, and my civilization, remembering my modest role in all of them. Then I would decide what to do next. I don't think I'll know until I'm in that position. God willing, that will never happen. No-a-Je, let's get back to work." The two men left the ready room.

After a few minutes, twelve crystal spiders moved from their hiding places and glowed light blue. They all flew down and landed on the commodores' desk, so that they were all touching each other. The team leader, Michamanades Nolobitamore added their strength to his in order to send his report to No-Makla. "Home world, this is team forty-seven. We are now two weeks out from No-Makla. We are making some progress in understanding these creatures, but not enough. Clearly this fleet has the power to attack our planet and we should be prepared. While we still do not understand their thoughts or spoken language, we can feel a great deal of indecision and confusion among the creatures. We will be in range to jump home in five days. Until then we will continue trying to learn their language. The issue from my last report is still very troubling. We are getting strong mind control messages on some of the ships. I am keeping my crew here since this ship seems unaffected. We are sensing at least three or four creatures that are sending those messages. I am very concerned these messages follow patterns similar to our communications. I do not know the source, but it is possible there are Predaxians on board one or more of these ships. Team forty-seven out." The creatures glowed white and disappeared.

CHAPTER 28

It took five days for Dave and Charlie to get back to the Io Space Port. He had to arrange for others to take his place managing the rebuilding of the Far Sky and New Dawn colonies. To keep his word to Drew and Corrine Baker, he asked Aria to jump back to Earth with Horace. He had been very disappointed that Jake had gone to Neptune, but understood the reasons. Horace had to bury his wife and their children on New Dawn as waves of disease swept through the colony. He missed each of them every day, and would be happy to have even one more minute with any of them again. Dave had also been required to provide detailed briefings on his encounter with the maklan to the team on Io as well as the High Councils of Kalidus and Earth.

On Io, his first priority was to meet with Bill and the team to hear how their work was going. It had not been a good meeting. Progress was painfully slow. The telepathic communication was too complex for them to decipher anything other than hints about emotions. When Dave told them about Jake, the team was very excited. They desperately wanted Jake to come and help them. Jake had already figured out how to communicate with humans. The Galliceans would never take a human interpreter's word for what the maklans said. They would need to hear it for themselves. When Dave told them that it took Jake one hundred years to learn to communicate with Horace Hildebrand, they were frustrated again. The Gallicean fleet was a week away from Jupiter. Fixing this communication problem seemed insurmountable. War was looking like the only probable outcome. Eight human and five Kalidean star cruisers orbited Mars, preparing for the fight. It would be a terrible day in the galaxy if fighting did break out. Dave began to wonder if sacrificing the maklans would be acceptable if it would save the galaxy.

The meeting went on for hour after hour with little or no good news. When dinner time arrived, Dave excused himself, hugged Bill and left the room. He could still hear arguments and tempers flaring as the door closed behind him. As he proceeded down the hallway, he heard a tone on his earpiece and pressed the contact. "Brother Dave," boomed the voice of Fa-a-Di, "I heard you were back in the vicinity. How are you, my dear friend?"

"Brother Fa-a-Di, it is good to hear your voice too," he replied. "I've wanted to ask you when we can fly together again? I don't know how much time we have left."

"Time is a pretty scarce resource right now, Brother," the general agreed. "That was indeed a great day for me as well. Your wife Darlene tells me you want to try Saturn this time. Is that true?"

"That is correct, Brother," Dave said.

"Tomorrow is a perfect day for me, Dave," Fa-a-Di laughed. "I am actually on my colony ship over Saturn right now. I will send the coordinates for our platform 1510 to your helmsman. It is a beautiful planet as well, but without the Dar-Fa, it is not quite so exciting. Will my brother Charlie be joining us? My brother-in-law De-o-Nu is arriving with the Kong-Fa within the hour. I'm sure he would love to join us."

"I'll ask, and I am certain he will agree," Dave replied. "Charlie talks to me about that adventure every time we talk, which is very often. I'm reading Io time at 1845 hours. Shall we meet at 0930 Io time tomorrow?"

"Perfect!" Fa-a-Di laughed. "Dave, before I disconnect, I did call for a reason. Can I tell you some good news?"

"Brother, I really need some good news now. Please continue," Dave answered.

"You know the Gallicean fleet will arrive in a few days. As I mentioned, De-o-Nu will arrive in an hour. He is not alone. There are a lot of Galliceans who are thoroughly loyal to me. They do not like what is happening on Gallia. We have talked about the High Council forcing me to retire. There are many odd things happening on Gallia these days. De-o-Nu is bringing his ship and fourteen other cruisers. Those captains are absolutely loyal to me and will not allow the war to happen. De-o-Nu is the only member of any of those crews who is from Gallia, so I am confident that they have not been contaminated by whatever is happening on our home planet."

Dave had stopped walking and was leaning against the wall of the ship, stunned by the words from his friend. "That is very good news indeed, friend," he stammered.

"It gets better Dave," the general continued. "Commodore Ka-a-Fa is leading the ten ships from Gallia which are supposed to destroy the Neptunians. I told him several of his crews are more loyal to me than to him or the Chiefs of Staff. I told Ka-a-Fa that six ships would join me. I know five for certain will. In my heart, I believe the sixth captain to join our side will be Ka-a-Fa himself. He has been fighting on the Predaxian frontier for many years. He knows what real war is all about. When he sees the situation with his own eyes, he will join us, I am sure of that."

"And if he doesn't, General?" Dave asked.

"Then our ships will destroy him and his ship," Fa-a-Di said. "Enough of this talk of war, brother. Have a good evening, and we will fly together tomorrow on Saturn. Rest well my friend. Saturn out." The line went dead.

Dave continued down the hallway. He had been headed for the dining hall, but was too overwrought by the events of the day and the call from the general. He changed course to return to his room. He pushed the door open and saw Darlene waiting for him with two glasses of red wine in her hands. He took her into his arms, kissed her and squeezed her tight, almost spilling the drinks.

An hour later, Dave and Darlene went to the dining hall for dinner. They sat across from each other, enjoying each other's companion far more than the food. While Dave had been dealing with the situation on New Dawn, Darlene had been working frantically to convince the Greater Gallia High Council to allow more time to be able to communicate with the Neptunians. The meetings continued for days with no headway. The Chiefs of Staff were asked to join the meetings after several days, and the negotiations become even more difficult. Field Marshall Je-e-Bo argued vehemently about the threat from the Neptunians. He told the group that he feared the Neptunians more than the Predaxian Alliance that continually harassed the outer Gallicean worlds. After five more days of argument, Mencius ended the negotiations before relations among the Galliceans, Kalideans and humans were put in jeopardy.

Dave and Darlene were about to leave the hall when Dave heard Jake's voice in his head. "Dave, it's Jake, can you hear me?" he thought.

"Did you hear that Dave?" asked Darlene. "Is that the Jake you told me about?"

"Jake," Dave thought, "Darlene can hear you too. Are you on No-Makla?"

Jake moved slightly so that they could see him sitting in the middle of their table, lightly touching them both. Darlene moved back suddenly, shocked by the creature's presence.

"It's okay, sweetheart," Dave told her. "Jake is harmless enough. Let him touch you so we can communicate." She moved her hand to be in contact with the invisible spider.

"Okay, Dave, I'm came here like I promised," Jake began. "I have lots of other news too. We had a team of maklans on one of the Gallicean cruisers in the fleet headed this way. They have spent weeks trying to understand them with little success. You remember it took me a hundred years to understand Horace."

"Yes, I remember Jake," Dave whispered. "Can you start working with our team now?"

"Yes, but our team has another plan, Dave. Even with our greatest minds working on this, in a few days we can never hope to learn what it took me a hundred years to learn. What we thought would help is if several maklans from that group studying the Galliceans could link with an actual Gallicean. A few more would link with you. I would link with you too. You would repeat everything the Gallicean says. The Gallicean would repeat everything you say. We maklans can link to each other without touching and share what we learn. We think if we had you two, with maybe fifty or a hundred maklans in the area, we could learn very fast. What do you think?" Jake asked.

"Do you think two humans and two Galliceans would make it ever better?" Dave asked.

"That would be a hundred times better Dave! Do you think you could do that?" Jake replied.

"It's already arranged Jake," Dave smiled. "Meet me in my quarters at 0800 hours local time."

CHAPTER 29

Dave, Darlene and Charlie were all sitting in Dave's quarters at 0800 hours the following morning. As usual, Charlie was responsible for bringing the coffee and pastries. Dave and Charlie were reminiscing about their flight on Jupiter when Dave heard Jake in his mind. "They're here," Dave said.

Twenty or more maklans appeared in the room and sat on the ceiling. Jake landed on the coffee table, extended a tendril into Dave's coffee and tasted it. "That's certainly not whisky, Dave. Ugh, it's terrible," Jake thought to them. Everyone laughed. "Michanamades here is my best friend and led the mission on the Gallicean ship," Jake thought as one of the creatures glowed pink for a second. "As you suggested, a group of a hundred maklans are currently on the platform over Saturn. Another twenty are on the colony ship above that planet. They have found the general's quarters and are hidden in there with him. What do we do now Dave?"

Dave reached forward and pushed a contact on his table top, saying, "Lia, please get General Fa-a-Di on the Gallicean colony ship and send his signal down here."

"Aye-aye, Admiral," she said.

A moment later the smiling beak of Fa-a-Di appeared on the screen. "Dave, I hope you are not calling to cancel. De-o-Nu and I are looking forward to this trip today," he said.

"Not a chance, Brother," Dave replied. "I do have a bit of a change in plans though. First, can you have De-o-Nu come to your quarters with you?"

"He's already on his way, Dave," he answered. "He was so excited he decided to jump here from the Kong-Fa and shuttle with me to the platform." The general's door opened and the familiar figure of Governor De-o-Nu appeared on the screen as well." "Brother, Dave was just asking about you? He wants to adjust our plans."

"Brother, you had better not cancel on me!" De-o-Nu shouted, "I've been anticipating this adventure since my brother-in-law told me last evening."

"We will be flying together soon, Brother," Dave answered. "But first I want you to meet my dear friend, Jake the maklan." Jake adjusted himself and glowed light blue so the others could see him.

"Remarkable," stammered Fa-a-Di. "A real Neptunian. Greetings little friend. Can Jake speak to us Dave?"

"Not yet, but that is why we are here now," he answered. "You probably heard from your scientists on Io that it took Jake a hundred years on New Dawn to understand humans. We don't have that much time. This is our only hope to avoid the war over Neptune. I need you two to trust me with your lives."

"Dave," De-o-Nu began, "to avoid this war, I will offer my life and those of my cruisers now circling Jupiter. My brother-in-law knows that is why we are all here. But what can we do?"

"Fly with Charlie and me over Saturn," Dave smiled.

"That hardly requires trust from us, Brother," Fa-a-Di said, "You will be the ones in harnesses connected to us."

"Do not react to what I am going to say, Brothers," Dave continued. "There are twenty maklans in the room with you now." The Galliceans looked around frantically. "Relax, they will do no harm. They are our friends."

"How will these creatures help us, Dave, if we cannot speak with them?" Fa-a-Di asked.

"That is why we are together now," Dave said. "After Charlie and I don our pressure suits, ten maklans will attach themselves to each of us. Ten maklans will attach to each of you as well. Don't worry, they will only be touching you, nothing more. Maklans have the ability to jump without a portal. Once we are ready, the maklans will jump with us to the platform. Be certain to wear your harnesses before we jump as there will be no need for a shuttle. On the platform, we can get into the harnesses and start our flight. We can go anywhere and do anything you want. The important point is you need to repeat everything we say to you, and we will do the same. The maklans will communicate with each other, using Jake as a leader. Since Jake understands humans, he will be able to help translate Gallicean words for them. Are you willing to try it, my brothers?"

Fa-a-Di said, "Without learning these things, there will be war, we can be certain of that. Even with this knowledge, there may still be war. Still, the only chance for peace is to do this. While we save the galaxy, we can fly together over Saturn. How can I say no to that?"

On Jake's thought, the twenty maklans in Fa-a-Di's room moved and glowed blue. After a moment of shock, both Galliceans laughed out loud. "Dave," Fa-a-Di said, "Signal us when you and Charlie are ready. Either we die or we live, together! Saturn out!"

Dave and Charlie scrambled into their pressure suits. Darlene checked the fittings and the readings on the suits and confirmed they were ready to go. She signaled Fa-a-Di they were ready. The maklans floated down from the ceiling and landed on Dave and Charlie. Dave heard Jake telling him to relax. The maklans glowed bright white and disappeared, leaving Darlene alone in the room.

The great expanse of Saturn stretched in every direction below them. The rings painted a path across the sky overhead. Dave could see the colony ship as a large dot, hundreds of miles above them. "You okay Charlie?" Dave asked.

"That's the only way to fly, buddy," he responded. They could see dozens of blue lights flying around the platform. Dave thought of his dream, knowing now that Neptune was the blue planet. A brilliant flash shone behind them and they turned to see Fa-a-Di and De-o-Nu appear from thin air on the platform.

"My God," the general shouted, "that was the most amazing experience of my life!" He unfolded his wings, happy to be out of the confines of his ship again. "Brother De-o-Nu, what did you think?"

"That is much better than a portal," he said. "Half of the time I get sick after a portal jump. Incredible!"

The maklans on Dave's suit lifted him off the platform and dropped him into the harness on Fa-a-Di. Jake personally checked all the locks and fittings. Then they did the same for Charlie. Jake thought, "You two are secure."

Dave said, "Thanks Jake. Brothers, we can't forget to repeat everything we hear from one another, or else the whole day will be wasted."

174

Fa-a-Di dutifully repeated Dave's words and added his own, "No day can be wasted when you explore a new planet with your brothers!" He dove off the platform into the atmosphere, soaring in the Saturnian sky. Charlie and De-o-Nu were right behind them. The group of maklans circled them and appeared to enjoy the flight themselves. After several minutes of flight, Fa-a-Di had a signal in his earpiece.

"General, we don't read you or the Governor on board," said the voice. "Are you okay?"

"You can read us both near platform 1510. We are busy and do not wish to be interrupted. Fa-a-Di out!" he finished.

CHAPTER 30

The Gallicean fleet was due to arrive at any time. Dave and Charlie sat nervously in the main meeting hall in the Io Star Port. They could see Fa-a-Di and De-o-Nu pacing impatiently on the other side of the glass separator. They were all there to meet with the team working on enabling communication between Galliceans and the maklans. The flyover of Saturn had been a tremendous help to get the work restarted. A number of maklans had joined the effort and worked with both sides to expand the vocabulary that had been learned that day. A tone sounded in Dave's earpiece followed by Lia's voice saying, "Admiral, we have the Gallicean star cruisers on our long range scanners. They should enter orbit over Neptune within three hours."

Dave responded, "Lia, please advise Fleet Admiral Arrin as well as the High Council. I recommend we move our fleet to Neptune as soon as possible."

The doors to the conference hall opened and the team entered. They seemed very happy on both sides of the glass as they made their ways to seats. The maklans fluttered about the room and settled onto the main table. Bill Brewster began, "Dear friends, it is our pleasure to report that the code for our translator devices has now been updated to include five thousand maklan words." The room erupted in applause. When it quieted, Bill continued, "Now, I would like to introduce Jacomofledes Benomafolays, our friend and colleague from No-Makla."

Dave could hear Jake saying "Greetings to all of you" through his earpiece. Jake continued, "This is a great day for No Makla. Our society has been peacefully traveling the galaxy for more than a billion Earth years, and today the circle of our friends has grown to include the humans, Galliceans and Kalideans. It is our great hope that the breakthrough from this team will insure our peoples can live together in peace. As you know, the Gallicean fleet is about to enter orbit around our home planet. Dr. No-o-Ka of Jupiter has already sent the updated code into the Gallicean information cloud, and we expect the translators on those ships to be updated by the time they arrive. We are counting on our dear friend, General Fa-a-Di to make certain that happens. He has much more influence in those matters than we do."

Fa-a-Di laughed heartily, saying, "You have my word friends. If they resist, De-o-Nu and I will personally deliver new translators and stick them in every captain's ears." He rose and began pacing, "We have to be realistic though. There is a real possibility that some of the ships will attack even with this wonderful news. There is blackness on the soul of Greater Gallia. Sometimes political expedience takes the place of common sense, and frivolous adventures can lead to the loss of life."

"Brother," De-o-Nu interrupted, "I have already sent my fleet to meet them at Neptune. They will arrive any time now, well ahead of Ka-a-Fa's ships."

"Thank you for that, Brother," Fa-a-Di continued, "I recommend the Earth and Kalidean ships do the same thing. We must make it clear to Ka-a-Fa there is no chance that he can succeed. When the taste of death is in his mouth, he will make the right choice. I am certain of that!"

Dave said, "Brothers, I have already given those orders. Our fleet will arrive over Neptune in the next hour. Charlie and I will be jumping to the Reliant after this meeting to join Cadiz."

"We will be on the Kong-Fa," the general said. "I know my brother-in-law always needs my help."

De-o-Nu laughed, "Dear brother, the hero of Nok-lak-a is always welcome on my bridge. And I'm not saying that because you outrank me, or because you are High Commissioner, or because I'm married to your sister." The room erupted in laughter.

Dave noticed the maklans had begun to glow red, and said, "Jake, what's wrong?"

"Dave, we can now sense the incoming Gallicean fleet. Michamanades Nolobitamore, who led the team that investigated the Dar-Fa told us they sensed some creatures similar to us on at least one of those ships. There are a few hundred maklans at the star port and we have enough of a common conscience that we can feel them now. There are Beings on three different ships that are not Galliceans," Jake reported.

"What!" shouted Fa-a-Di. "What kind of creatures are they? Why haven't our crews noticed them? This is all very unusual, Jake. Are you sure of this?"

"We are certain, General," Jake replied. "I have also been signaled from No-Makla where there are billions of us. Our High Council confirmed three Predaxians on board those ships."

De-o-Nu jumped to his feet, shouting, "Predaxians! This is an outrage. Our crews would never allow Beings from the Predaxian Alliance to board our ships. There must be an error."

Jake spoke calmly, "Governor, there is no error. Please know the creatures from Predax are like maklans in many ways. Predax was colonized by the same Beings that colonized Neptune. But that was a billion Earth years ago. Both species have changed since then, but they can be as hard to detect as we were in your quarters over Saturn. Over the millennia, the maklans from Predax lost their ability to communicate telepathically and to fly.

Their telepathy evolved into mind control. Believe me there is no such thing as a Predaxian Alliance. Those maklans have created an empire by taking over the leader's minds on the planets they conquered. The maklans of Ai-Makla, our home world were peaceful explorers like the maklans of No-Makla. On Predax, they became obsessed with power and expansion. The maklans of Predax could never pilot large star cruisers and invade planets. They are frail and small like me. However, they have plenty of other races under their control who can."

"General," Dave said, "are you thinking what I am thinking?"

"Neptune is a diversion," Fa-a-Di said softly, slumping down into his chair. "Ka-a-Fa is under Predaxian control and will attack Neptune. While all of these ships are battling over nothing here, the Alliance will invade Greater Gallia."

Jake glowed white and disappeared, only to reappear in front of Fa-a-Di. "General, there were no Predaxians on the Dar-Fa. We have confirmed that. Commodore Ka-a-Fa has not been compromised. We do have to assume that three other ship's captains are under Predaxian control. Without a doubt, those three ships will attack No-Makla."

"Those three ships will be easily destroyed by our fleet and the seven other ships in Ka-a-Fa's fleet. He will not allow any treason within his fleet," De-o-Nu said.

"That is probably true Governor," Jake continued. "You must remember only the captain and perhaps a couple other Galliceans are under Predaxian control on each ship. A single Predaxian maklan cannot control all the minds on a ship. You would be killing many people who had no malicious intent. We do have a plan, but there is another complication."

180

"I assumed it would not be easy, my friend," Fa-a-Di sighed. "Besides an invasion of Greater Gallia and attack on harmless maklans, what is the other complication?"

Jake replied, "When we flew over Saturn, you told us about the situation on Gallia. We are always concerned when Beings act unusually. If one person acts oddly, that could be insanity or a medical condition. When groups of people change their behavior simultaneously, that is a strong sign of mind control. A group of two hundred maklans jumped to your home world. That team confirmed the presence of dozens of Predaxian maklans throughout the capitol city. As we had expected, each member of your Chiefs of Staff appears to be under the control of a Predaxian."

Fa-a-Di adjusted himself uneasily in his chair. "I suppose I should have guessed that," he groaned. "What about this solution you have in mind?"

"General, we will need you, your brother-in-law and four other Galliceans whom you will trust with the future of our worlds," Jake finished.

CHAPTER 31

Ka-a-Fa and his fleet arrived and entered orbit over Neptune on schedule. He was amazed to see the number of ships already in orbit. Ne-o-Ka advised him that fourteen Gallicean, eight Earth, and five Kalidean star cruisers were in orbit. "Ne-o-Ka," he said, "hail General Fa-a-Di."

The general's smiling face appeared on the view screen almost immediately. He was wearing his battle uniform with laser blasters on each hip and three daggers in his belt. Fa-a-Di remained an intimidating figure after many years in politics. "Commodore Ka-a-Fa, welcome to the Earth star system! I trust all is well with your region of the Predaxian frontier."

"My last report I received said it was very quiet. That is a blessing for me, as you know," the commodore replied. "We are awaiting final orders from the Chiefs of Staff. Would you like to join me on the Dar-Fa for a glass of whisky while we wait?"

Fa-a-Di smiled, "No, I don't think that would be a good idea. I trust your fleet has connected to the Gallicean cloud and updated its systems as per standard protocol?"

"Of course we have, General. I am not a child," Ka-a-Fa scoffed. "We have listened to the report from Dr. No-o-Ka about the peaceful intentions of the maklans of Neptune. That's all well and good, but as you have properly told me, a soldier follows orders."

"Yes, that is true Brother," Fa-a-Di laughed. "I think I told you I would court-martial you myself if you did not. Life is complicated though. A man must do the right thing to bring honor to his family and save his soul. Only a fool follows the orders of a madman."

"Who is mad then, General? You, Je-e-Bo, perhaps me?" Ka-a-Fa laughed. "I am a simple man. I can't . . . General, I'm getting a signal from the Chiefs of Staff. We can talk later. Dar-Fa out!" The scowling faces of the three Chiefs appeared in front of him and his bridge crew.

"Sirs, we are in orbit over Neptune," Ka-a-Fa said. "My fleet is at your disposal. As you have no doubt been told, we have been joined by twenty-two other war ships that recommend we do not attack that planet."

Je-e-Bo screamed, "Commodore, the Chiefs of Staff are not intimidated by those fools. We have reconfirmed your orders with the High Council. Those creatures on Neptune will take over Greater Gallia if you fail to act now. Attack now or you will be replaced!" Three heavily armed guards jumped onto the bridge with blasters at the ready to insure Ka-a-Fa followed his orders.

"Aye-aye, Field Marshal," Ka-a-Fa said quietly as the screen went dark. "Ne-o-Ka, order the fleet into attack formation." He closed his eyes and sighed heavily. He turned to his crew, saying, "Today is a good day to die, my friends. May God be with us."

All thirty-two ships over Neptune began to move and establish their positions. Ka-a-Fa's fleet formed a double delta formation with each group of ships focused on a different population center. De-o-Nu's fleet jumped into action, crossing the other ships' paths to draw them into dogfights. The Earth ships were heavily outgunned and stayed close to the Kalidean ships for protection. The Kalideans stationed themselves in the path of the oncoming attackers.

Ka-a-Fa said, "Ne-o-Ka, let's focus on the Kong-Fa. The General and Governor are probably foolish enough to be there together. If we can knock her out of the fight, the rest might surrender."

"The Governor's ship is not within the enemy fleet, sir," Ne-o-Ka responded.

The commodore was dumbfounded. "Those are his ships about to be destroyed out there and he's hiding? I cannot believe that. Find that ship!" he screamed.

The first group of attackers was rapidly approaching the city of Nokalamalon, home to four hundred million maklans. As they fired, the Kalidean ship, Validus jumped in front of their fire. Her defense screens absorbed most of the blasts, although they were now without protection and had to withdraw for repair. The Defiant was also hit by the blast and was severely damaged. Her captain sent out a distress signal and the Courage raced to tow her out of danger.

Ka-a-Fa's group of ships was nearing target distance to Amarofledes, the maklan capitol city, with one billion citizens. He was about to order the group to fire when three nearby Gallicean ships attacked. The Dar-Fa was hit hard, and smoke filled the bridge. They took evasive action to get out of the way while the other four ships attacked. Explosions and fire erupted in the maklan city. When the bridge cleared of smoke, Ka-a-Fa could see that five of his crew were dead, including the three guards. He ordered his ships to regroup for the next attack run.

"Commodore, we have an incoming message from Governor Mak-Kal-a of the Nom-Kat-La colony," Ne-o-Ka said as he wiped blood off of his face.

"You fool," the commodore shouted, "can't you see we are busy now? Tell them to wait."

"But Commodore," Ne-o-Ka insisted, "the Governor is saying the Alliance has invaded his region and there are a hundred ships now bombarding his planet. At least two hundred thousand invaders have landed within the last ten minutes."

Ka-a-Fa was stunned and was lost in thought for a minute. "Call off the attack immediately, Ne-o-Ka," the commodore said as he slumped in his chair. He had also just noticed he was bleeding from his head. "And get me Fa-a-Di immediately!" His fleet immediately withdrew from Neptune and moved to higher orbits, out of range of the other ships.

De-o-Nu's smiling face appeared on the Dar-Fa's view screen. "Commodore, my old friend, it is a surprise to hear from you now. My brother-in-law is not here, but I will listen to your last words or your surrender if you like."

"Brother, we have been had," Ka-a-Fa began, "I have just been told the Alliance has invaded our frontier and are now attacking Nom-Kat-La. The Chiefs have told me to attack, but in my heart, I know I must stop the invasion."

"We know brother," De-o-Nu said. "The maklans of Neptune told us this would probably happen. We have already arranged for all of our ships to use the Io portal to go directly to Nom-Kat-La and join the real fight. As you can imagine, I will not leave you here to attack the maklans. If you jump, my fleet will follow yours."

"But Brother, your ship is not even here. Are you hiding the Kong-Fa while you shiver in fear?" Ka-a-Fa laughed.

"The Kong-Fa is very close, Ka-a-Fa," De-o-Nu smiled. "We have a specific mission on orders from High Commissioner Fa-a-Di. We will join the fray at the appropriate time. After your ships and mine jump through the portal, I will follow closely behind. I would be honored to die with you today over Nom-Kat-La, brother. There is no honor to be gained for you or Greater Gallia over Neptune."

"Ne-o-Ka, signal our ships to travel to Io at top speed and jump through the portal there," the commodore said so that De-o-Nu could hear. "Brother, I will lead the way, and be waiting for you on the field of battle." The Dar-Fa sped away from Neptune at top speed. As had been suspected, six other ships from his fleet followed quickly behind. Following their orders, the fourteen ships from De-o-Nu's fleet and the battle-ready Kalidean and Earth ships left orbit and followed Ka-a-Fa.

Captain Fo-o-Ba of the San-Fa hailed the other remaining ships, saying, "Gentlemen, we have work to do. Each of you should target as many cities as you can and blast the Neptunians! The glory of Greater Gallia is in our hands!" The three ships broke formation and dived toward the planet. The ships fired randomly with little concern for accuracy. The planet lay helplessly in their paths.

De-o-Nu appeared from thin air on the bridge of the San-Fa in full battle gear. At the same moment, his lieutenants No-ka-De and Nan-de-Bo appeared on the bridges of the other two ships. De-o-Nu shouted, "Fo-o-Ba, prepare to enter the gates of hell!" as he aimed and fired the blaster in his left hand at the captain's chest. The bridge crew was too shocked to react, fumbling with their side-arms. The stun blast hit the captain and he fell backward and crashed to the floor. The whole room could see the Predaxian maklan become visible when it became disconnected from the captain. It was about twice the size of the maklans on

187

Neptune with a reddish shell and twelve long arms. It scrambled for cover. Jake, who was riding on De-o-Nu's chest told him to fire. De-o-Nu pulled the blaster from his right holster and fired a full blast at the creature which screamed in pain and collapsed. Jake told De-o-Nu that the Predaxian was dead.

The crew on the bridge was shocked, but had now trained their weapons on De-o-Nu, who dropped his blasters to the ground. Fo-o-Ba rose, waving off his crew, saying, "De-o-Nu, what are you doing in this region? Why has my crew raised their weapons on you? Shouldn't you be on Jupiter?"

General Fa-a-Di and his two lieutenants appeared at the same moment in the office of the Chiefs of Staff. Field Marshal Je-e-Bo screamed, "What treason is this, Fa-a-Di?" Before any of the Chiefs could summon security, Fa-a-Di's and his men blasted the three, knocking their Predaxian parasites to the ground. The Predaxians were quickly killed with the full blasts. Before security could react to the attack, their attached maklans jumped them back to Jupiter.

CHAPTER 32

The breadth of the Neptunian atmosphere spread below them. Dave Brewster was completely at home in the harness with Fa-a-Di. De-o-Nu spiraled around them with Charlie Watson along for the ride. The Galliceans had to wear heavy clothing to protect them from the frigid air so far from the sun. The planet was so blue it felt like they were flying through an ocean. Countless blue lights circled them as a crowd of maklans joined the fun. Dave could see the lights of Amarofledes in the distance ahead of them. He knew Darlene was there with High Commissioner Darak working on partnership treaties with the No-Makla High Council.

"Brother Fa-a-Di," Dave said at last, "I will miss our flights when you return to Gallia."

"Me too brother," the High Commissioner said. "The Chiefs of Staff have demanded I remain High Commissioner until the Predaxian problem is resolved. When they learned how easily the Predaxian maklans had penetrated our defenses and taken control of their bodies, they could not believe it. Je-e-Bo and I have a long history of fighting together and we long for the opportunity again. You know you have a standing offer to fly on Gallia with me. It would be amazing since we would probably have a crowd of ten or twenty thousand Galliceans with us."

"Don't forget me either, brother," Charlie said. "De-o-Nu and I want to be part of the fun."

"That's right, brother-in-law," De-o-Nu added. "I am grateful I am allowed to join Ka-a-Fa on the front lines, but I will miss Jupiter and Saturn. And I will miss our maklan friends as well!" The maklans glowed blue in happiness.

189

"Don't worry, guys," Jake replied as he spiraled around the group. "With your ships and our capabilities, we will win the day with the Predaxians. We have already recruited a hundred thousand maklans to jump to Nom-Kat-La and Gallia to help uncover them. We will always be there to help you after what you have done for us."

"We should arrive at Amarofledes soon," Fa-a-Di said. "Hopefully there will be a banquet waiting for us. I'm so hungry I could eat a cow! That's the right word, right Dave?"

Dave laughed, "That's right brother." Dave looked over at Charlie, slung under De-o-Nu. "Charlie, you want to know something."

"Sure Dave, what's that?" Charlie replied.

Dave sighed and said, "The best day of my life is when I left my wallet in my car."

The group continued to fly off toward the great city and another adventure.

ABOUT THE AUTHOR

Karl J. Morgan

Karl Morgan grew up fascinated by science fiction, beginning with Victor Appleton's Tom Swift novels that he read as a young boy. Later, he became enthralled with the works of his favorite author, Isaac Asimov, especially his Foundation series.

Those early experiences inspired his life-long love of science fiction and interest in hard science, focusing first on astronomy and later cosmology and quantum mechanics. Karl had the great honor to take his first astronomy course at the University of Iowa from the legendary scientist, Dr. James Van Allen. More recently, the brilliant works of Drs. Stephen Hawking, Brian Greene, and Michio Kaku helped him understand that our physical universe is still a magical and mysterious place.

It is that sense of magic and mystery that brings Karl to write about his alter ego, Dave Brewster, an unemployed accountant who finds himself a thousand years in the future with new friends and adventures far beyond anything he could have imagined. There, he can find answers to questions that befuddle mankind today. The truth he finds is no different from what we know today. Life is always about loving and caring for our family and friends.

Karl lives in San Diego with his wife, Aida and their beloved puppies. Their two grown children have fled the nest and started their own adventures in life.

OTHER BOOKS BY
KARL J. MORGAN

Remembrances: Choose to Be Happy and Embrace the Possibilities
ISBN: 978-0-9826461-9-9

The Dave Brewster Series

The Dave Brewster Series: The Second Predaxian War
(Book 2)
ISBN: 978-0-9860270-1-7
Available for purchase early 2013

The Dave Brewster Series: The Hive
(Book 3)
ISBN: 978-0-9860270-2-4
Available for purchase early 2013

The Dave Brewster Series: Tears of Gallia
(Book 4)
ISBN: 978-0-9860270-4-8
Available for purchase early Spring 2013

Heartstone

Heartstone: Sentinels of Far Sun
ISBN: 978-0-9860270-3-1
Available for purchase early Spring 2013

www.ingramcontent.com/pod-product-compliance
Lightning Source LLC
Chambersburg PA
CBHW070026120726
47909CB00003B/1069